Sherlock Holmes and the Roswell Incident

By Michael Druce

Paperback ISBN 978-1-78705-298-7
ePub ISBN 978-1-78705-299-4
PDF ISBN 978-1-78705-300-7

Published in the UK by MX Publishing
335 Princess Park Manor, Royal Drive,
London, N11 3GX
www.mxpublishing.com

Cover layout and construction by
Brian Belanger

Author's Note

With few exceptions, I am a fan of both the literary and film adventures of Sherlock Holmes. For me, Holmes and Watson are timeless and ageless. Thus, I enjoy the various iterations of Sherlock Holmes stories no matter when and where they are set. I take pleasure in the works of Conan Doyle set in the 1800s as well as the films of Basil Rathbone set during World War II, the Robert Downey Jr. adventures, and the contemporary *Sherlock*.

In *Sherlock Holmes and the Roswell Incident*, Holmes and Watson exist in a later time than that of the original stories. My hope is readers are forgiving of my taking such creative license.

When one blends factual events with fiction, persons, places, and events are necessarily subject to cherry picking. Some remain in service to the story, some are embellished, and others are ignored entirely. Where no factual record exists, one may conclude these are the invention of the author. Errors of fact may also be attributed to the author.

M.D.

FORWARD

On Halloween night 1938, a brash young actor and producer by the name of Orson Welles created a scandal that would have repercussions for years to come. The young Welles and his Mercury Theatre troupe mounted a daring radio production of H. G. Wells' *War of the Worlds*. Departing from the narrative of the novel, the production was broadcast as a series of simulated news bulletins. Airing with a disclaimer that the program to follow was a radio fiction, many listeners who tuned in late missed the warning and believed they were listening to an eyewitness report of an actual Martian invasion. The broadcast caused hysteria nationwide and created a public relations nightmare for the Columbia Broadcasting System. The broadcast should have ruined the career of the upstart Orson Welles. Instead, it had quite the opposite effect. Welles expressed the appropriate humility and regret, yet one could not help but sense he was delighted by the attention. Soon thereafter he became the recipient of Hollywood's Holy Grail, a contract to make motion pictures. For a short time, Welles was proclaimed as Hollywood's *boy wonder*. His fame was meteoric. But as often happens in Hollywood, ego, money, and politics took their toll and the young Welles quickly flamed out.

Due in part perhaps to the apprehension of an impending war and the paranoia associated with uncertainty, the fears that had been exposed by the radio broadcast never entirely vanished. They slipped below the surface of the public's consciousness, and there they would remain until some years hence when they would once again be brought to the surface by what would become known as UFO fever.

How Sherlock Holmes and I found ourselves ensnared in what yet remains the most famous UFO mystery of all time, I now set forth in the adventure I call *Sherlock Holmes and the Roswell Incident.*

CHAPTER 1
All good things

London, 1946

Thursday fortnights for almost a year, Ellen Sharpe arrived by train at Victoria Station. With a large leather bag slung over her shoulder, she exited the train, threaded her way through the cavernous station, and walked five minutes to an obscure little restaurant called *The Thesean Thread*. The young woman who was considered a regular was warmly greeted by the proprietor and led to her preferred table by the window overlooking Ebury Street. Her habit was to sit with her back to the window to avoid being recognized. Practically speaking, her preferred table allowed easy access to the exit.

A waiter brought Ellen Sharpe's drink order on a small tray.

She thanked him with a smile and stared into the glass, losing herself in a kaleidoscope of memories.

A shadow fell across the table.

"Do you mind if I join you?"

Ellen Sharpe glanced up at a familiar face. It was not the face she was expecting to see. For an instant, her heart stopped beating. A hundred thoughts raced through her mind. She drew a breath and smiled graciously. Mustering as much poise as she was able, she did not wish to belie the fear that had suddenly taken hold.

"By all means. Please."

The man sat across from her. As matter of habit, he smoothed his tie, although it wasn't necessary. He was impeccably tailored.

"Intriguing name, don't you think? *The Thesean Thread.*"

"Is it? I can't imagine I have given it much thought."

"Reminds one of the labyrinth, Theseus, the Minotaur, Icarus. Suggestive of all sorts of intrigue and possibility, wouldn't you agree?"

"As I say, it is not something I have considered. I come here because it is quiet and friendly. It is a pleasant atmosphere in which to have a drink after a day of work."

A waiter approached. "Your usual, sir?"

The man nodded.

The waiter thanked the gentleman and hurried away.

"Creature of habit, I am afraid. Since discovering this quaint little place, I come here often. Funny how predictable we become, how easily we slip into routines."

Ellen Sharpe managed a thin smile. She moved her leg against the large leather bag resting against the left side of her chair.

"Sometimes others recognize our routines before we ourselves do."

"I really couldn't say."

"Miss Sharpe, isn't it?"

"Ellen," the young woman replied.

"Of course."

The waiter returned with the gentleman's drink.

"Another?" Ellen's intrusive guest asked.

Ellen Sharpe shook her head. "Thank you, but no."

The waiter was dismissed with a curt gesture.

"You are with de Havilland, I believe."

Ellen nodded.

"You have been with them since ...?"

"Forty-four," Ellen said quietly.

"Forty-four. Yes, shortly before the end of the war. A lot of fine work being done at de Havilland. Cutting edge, I believe they say, especially the Comet project. A first-class piece of aeronautical technology. During the war, de Havilland saved our proverbial bacon. You know the Germans were keen to wipe that place off the face of the planet. They undertook a sustained campaign to bomb it right out of existence. It was because of that pesky DH 98 Mosquito. It turns out those wooden wonders gave the Germans fits. I don't suppose you were onboard during the effort to make it appear as if the Germans had succeeded in destroying the de Havilland facility. It was all very theatrical and quite successful, I should say."

"That happened before my time."

"Quite right. You are a draughtswoman, I believe."

Ellen Sharpe nodded.

"That must be extraordinarily interesting, drafting designs, reproducing copies of components. I should think it must be tremendously rewarding work for a young woman such as yourself."

"Very. I am most grateful to have gotten a berth with the company."

"But I shouldn't imagine it pays well."

"I make ends meet."

"As it would seem. That is a lovely necklace you are wearing."

"Thank you." Ellen's fingers instinctively felt for the pendant around her neck. The flesh beneath her fingers felt as if it would burst into flame. She wondered if her neck were turning red.

"It must be difficult to afford such a beautiful piece of jewelry on a draughtswoman's salary."

"It was a gift."

"Paris, wasn't it?"

Ellen's heart sank.

"Paris, where nothing is more fantastic, more tragic, more sublime."

Ellen Sharpe knew her Victor Hugo. The moment this unwanted guest had asked to join her, she had hoped against all hope his presence was merely a courtesy or a meaningless flirtation.

"What was his name again?"

Ellen smiled to herself. This encounter was a fishing expedition. They didn't know her lover's name; nor would they find out.

The man waited.

Obstinately, Ellen stared directly into the man's eyes.

"Such nobility in loyalty. And yet loyalty is so often misplaced. No matter. Eventually everything rises to the surface. I gather we will find equally important information in that leather bag at your feet."

Ellen's thoughts drifted back to the two brief holidays she had spent in Paris with her Russian lover. He had swept her off her feet and showered her with gifts and affection. He had asked so little in return for a few brief days of bliss.

"Ironically, his majesty's government has received an order from the Soviet Union for twenty Nene and Derwent engines. What is one to make of that? It makes a perfect mockery of industrial espionage when one's own government is selling the very secrets one has been smuggling abroad."

Ellen had nothing to say.

"Should you be curious, the contact you normally meet here has another engagement. But, of course, you have already gathered that. When you think about it, isn't it all water under the bridge? You really don't expect to

4

see your paramour again, do you? Why not make it easy on yourself? Give us his name."

"I cannot."

"Miss Sharpe, I implore you to look out for yourself. The Soviets are notorious for taking advantage of vulnerable young women and then disposing of them. You deserve better."

Ellen slowly pushed away from the table.

"No rush. Take your time. Finish your drink. When you are ready, two gentlemen are here to escort you to SIS headquarters."

Mycroft Holmes rose from the table.

"Good evening, Miss Sharpe."

Ellen Sharpe stared into her glass, recalling that all too brief time with Arkady. How sad, she thought, never to see him again.

CHAPTER 2
Fire in the sky

Roswell, New Mexico
July 7, 1947

A fireball illuminated the night sky over New Mexico as if daylight had veered from its diurnal course and returned whence it came. Thousands witnessed the fiery object streak across the night sky above Roswell before it eventually crashed to earth some seventy-five miles away. Telephone switchboards throughout the region lit up like Christmas trees, suddenly ablaze with inquiries and breathless reports of a fiery crash. Radio stations were inundated with calls. The Army Air Forces were put on alert as a matter of routine. Events such as this attracted widespread public attention; however, little of what happened was rare or unusual. No one at the Roswell Army Air Field was overly concerned. A severe thunderstorm had passed through earlier that evening. Few were anxious to begin a search for what was most likely a meteorite. Dozens of similar incidents had been reported over the years. Most often they yielded nothing. Either they remained undiscovered or they had burned themselves to ash. Rarely did one find anything other than cold molten rock.

This night an amorous young couple was engaged in an activity referred to as *parking*. To ensure their privacy, the young couple had driven to a secluded location to vent their passions. The young man and the young lady had both recently graduated high school. They had been sweethearts for three years. In addition to acting upon those pent-up passions, this night of parking had also been planned to decide their futures. Should marriage come first and then college? Or should it be college and then marriage? Or should it be marriage and college at the same time? The young man was leaning toward marriage first. The young lady, the more levelheaded of the two, preferred college first.

In the middle of a heated embrace, the fireball roared overhead. The object was so close the couple could have sworn it scraped the roof of the car. Everything lit up around them as if a million cameras had flashed at one time. The noise was that of a train roaring past. The heat was instant and intense. The tires of the car exploded, and the rubber windshield wipers vaporized, leaving nothing but runny, black ooze.

The girl pulled away from her boyfriend and quickly re-buttoned her blouse. "Good God, Lee, what was that? Was it a plane?"

Lee slid across the seat to the driver's side and pushed open the door. "I don't know. I'm about to burn up. I've got to get out of here."

Several hundred yards on an intense fire cast an orange glow across the rough New Mexico terrain. The boy leaned into the driver's side window.

"Get me my flashlight. It's in the glove box. Whatever it is, it crashed just over there."

The girl had switched on the dome light and was looking at the right side of her face in the rearview mirror.

"Jenny, I said get me the flashlight!"

The girl pressed her hand to one cheek and then the other. "The right side of my face is burned."

"Grab my light. Let's have a look."

Jenny removed the torch from the glove compartment and exited the vehicle on the passenger's side. She walked around the car to her boyfriend. "Here," she said, handing the torch to the shaken young man.

Lee shone the light on Jenny's right cheek. "Gee, it's like you've got a sunburn on one side of your face. What about me?"

Jenny took the torch and shined it in Lee's face. "The whole left side of your face is completely red. We need to get home."

"No," Lee said, looking toward the now waning orange glow. "I want to know what that is."

"Lee, we should get back to Roswell as soon as we can. We need to get to a hospital. These burns might be serious."

"I am not leaving until I know what that is."

"It's not our business. Now let's go!"

Lee glanced first at his front tire, and then the rear, and then he circled his car. "We're not going anywhere."

"Fine," Jenny snapped. "I'll take the car and you can stay here."

"Jenny, the tires are blown out."

Jenny glanced down at the smoldering tires. "Do you have a spare?"

"Not four of them, I don't!"

"You don't have to bite my head off. I'll walk up to the highway then," the girl said.

"You think that's a smart idea in the dark?"

"Have you got a better idea?"

"I'm sorry, I didn't mean to snap at you. I'm sure someone will be out this way soon. We're not the only ones who saw this. Other people will have seen that fire in the distance. It couldn't be more than a few hundred yards from here."

"Lee, I don't want to get into trouble. You know how my momma can be, if she finds out."

"Jenny, we're already in trouble. We're not leaving here until somebody drives us home. You don't think my dad is going to be upset about his car? Come on, let's see what this thing is."

"I hope you know what you're doing."

"You and me both."

Following the beam of light from his torch, Lee took Jenny by the hand and led her toward the glow in the distance.

When the young couple reached the impact site, the flames had drawn down. Lee and Jenny stepped into a smoky clearing. Brush and scrubland trees were now smoky skeletons. The burning object began to collapse into itself.

"What is this, Lee?"

"It ain't no meteor."

"Is it a plane?" The girl asked.

Lee squeezed Jenny's hand. "Not like any plane I've seen. At least I don't think it is. It's so bent and twisted it's hard to say. It's some sort of craft. What else could it be?"

"This is spooky, Lee. I think we should go."

At that moment something rustled in the bushes on the other side of the object. Jenny squeezed Lee's hand so hard he felt as if his fingers would break.

"What is that?" Jenny whispered.

The young couple peered into the darkness. For an instant there was a white light, as if someone with a torch was among the rocks beyond the burn site.

Lee aimed his torch in the direction of the light. Immediately the other light disappeared. Then he pointed his torch at the area from which the noise had come. Jenny screamed, her hand flying up to her mouth.

Two creatures were moving toward them and then froze, as if startled by Lee's torch and Jenny's scream. One of the creatures leaned against a rock for support. It seemed to be gasping for air. The other

9

creature dropped to the ground on all fours. It too seemed to be gasping for air. Whatever these creatures were, they were unlike anything the couple had ever seen before. They were humanoid in form, each with two arms and two legs and facial features, but they were not human. They appeared reptilian.

"What are they, Lee? Are they hurt?" Jenny asked nervously.

"I don't know, and I don't want to find out. We should get out of here."

As the couple turned to run in the direction from which they had come, three cars careened through the brush and tumbleweed and came to an earth-gouging stop in front of the pair. Doors flew open and slammed shut. Two blinding beams of light engulfed the young couple. "Stay where you are," a voice commanded.

***

Abe Carl was deep in the mine when the ground rumbled. Beams above his head shook. Lights flickered. Loose dirt and rock peppered down all around him. "What the hell?" He mumbled to himself. If that was a tremor, he thought, another could come any second. Best to err on the side of caution. He packed it in for the night and made his way up to the entrance of the mine.

He stepped into the crisp night and gulped down two lungs full of what should have been clean, fresh air. Only there wasn't anything clean or fresh about it. The air was thick and smoky. "Fire," he said to himself. Unusual since a heavy rain had moved through earlier. A fire burning on a night like this would be intense. He wiped the dust from his face with his bandana and peered toward the line of scrubs along the Eastern boundary of his ranch. He referred to his place as a ranch, but it was hardly that. Mostly it was a dry, windblown, fifty acres of tumbleweeds and shifting sand. His land hadn't been a ranch for a good ten years. He didn't own any livestock or raise much of anything other than a few vegetables. Abe had been a widower for as long as he had owned the ranch. The ranch was an insurance settlement intended to compensate him for the loss of the woman he had married at seventeen. No question the ranch had helped the old man fill his days chipping out a living in the mine extracting iridium, but it had not made up for the absence of the woman he had loved.

Iridium is a rare element commonly associated with meteorites. That it should be found in the Earth's crust has given rise to speculation that it is not naturally occurring. Many in the science community believe iridium is the result of a massive meteorite impacting the Earth almost seventy million years ago. Some scientists went so far as to suggest that meteor could have been responsible for the extinction of the dinosaurs. Abe Carl couldn't speak to that, nor was he much interested. What he knew of iridium was that it was an extremely dense element that had value in the science and medical communities. It was well suited for use in thermoelectric generators, spark plugs, and crucibles. It also earned him a modest annual income.

The fire appeared to be burning down. From Abe's vantage point it didn't appear threatening. Out here there was little damage a fire could do. Most likely it was a meteorite. Still, Abe thought he ought to have a look. You never knew. He grabbed an axe and a torch and made his way toward the orange glow flickering through the scrubs.

Moving through a cluster of burned and hewn down brush, Abe came upon the source of the flames. He drew a breath and steadied himself with the axe handle.

He had not stumbled onto a meteorite at all; he had come upon a crash site. Bits and pieces of torn and twisted metal were scattered about. Was it a plane? If so, it wasn't like any aircraft he had seen before. It was a disc, saucer shaped. The outer layer of the craft's skin had burned away leaving only a twisted and rapidly collapsing skeleton. Ever since the war ended, there had been rumors of top-secret aircraft over the skies of New Mexico and Nevada. Perhaps this was one of those. Suddenly something spooked him. There was movement and the rustling of crushed brush. Abe turned on his light and pointed it in the direction of the sound. Two beings came into view. Abe's heart skipped a beat. "Good God," he said to himself. Whatever he was looking at, they were not human. The two beings froze. They appeared disoriented and confused. Abe held tight to his axe. He wasn't sure if they would attack or flee. Raising his axe for protection, the two creatures turned away from Abe and fled back in the direction from which they had come. Abe aimed his light into the brush. At once another light from the other side of the crash site appeared. Quickly Abe turned off his light. There were others. Why? Why would others be out here in the middle of nowhere? Whatever that burning object was and whatever those creatures were, Abe knew he had stumbled onto something he shouldn't have. Before he had time to think, several cars appeared from nowhere and raced toward the fire. Headlights glowed across the scrublands. The two creatures, one now leaning against a rock and the other on the ground, were silhouetted in the glare of headlights. Soon additional, more intense lights illuminated the area. Abe thought he could make out two additional figures between the headlights and the waning fire, but he couldn't be sure. Whatever was going on, it was big. The sudden appearance of cars and people running around had to mean government officials, and Abe didn't trust the government. He had heard plenty of strange stories over the years. You hear enough of them and you begin to think there's something to them. His was the only ranch in the immediate area. It wouldn't be long before the suits came knocking at his door. He knew of cases where people got into trouble just minding their own business, and here he was a potential witness to something he was sure he was not supposed to see. He needed to protect himself. He needed to share what he had seen with someone else. He knew exactly who to call. He had a friend at the *Roswell Daily Record*. For the time being, he'd keep the part about the creatures to himself. There might be a perfectly plausible explanation that he hadn't considered. But the burning wreck, that was a saucer all right. No doubt about that.

Taking care not to be seen, Abe Carl quietly slipped away from the crash site and returned to his little house near the mine. After pouring himself a stiff drink, he telephoned his friend at the newspaper.

***

"Stay right where you are! If you move, we will shoot!"

The young couple froze in place, reaching for each other's hand.

From the glare of the blinding lights, two men emerged. The taller of the two was dressed in a military uniform; the other man wore a suit. The man in the suit looked toward the lights and dragged a finger across his throat. Lee and Jenny closed their eyes, believing the worst was about to happen. Immediately the lights of both automobiles dimmed.

Jenny was sure her heart had stopped.

13

"Who are you?" Lee asked nervously.

"We ask the questions," the taller of the two men replied. "What are you doing out here?"

"We saw the fire. We thought it might have been a crash."

"It wasn't a crash," the man in the suit said.

"But there's wreckage everywhere," Jenny said. "You can see it for yourself."

"There is no wreckage. This is an ordinary fire started by a lightning strike. Understood?"

Lee and Jenny looked at each other and then at the two men. They nodded their heads.

"Good, we understand each other," the man in the uniform said. "I am Major White. This is Mr. Black."

"There's a car a couple of hundred yards back. Is it yours?" Mr. Black asked.

"Yes," Lee said.

"Where are you two from?"

"Roswell," Jenny replied.

"Roswell? That's damn near eighty miles away. What the hell are you doing all the way out here?"

"We spent the afternoon at my grandparent's place in Corona."

"Which doesn't explain what you are doing out here."

"We were parking," Jenny burst out. "We stopped to make out for a while. That's when we saw the fireball, I mean, the lightning storm that started the fire."

"You both of age?" Mr. Black asked.

"Look, who are you guys? Are we in trouble because we're parking?" Lee asked.

"We are both eighteen," Jenny said.

"We don't care about that. We are concerned, however, about how clear you are about what happened here tonight."

"We're clear," Jenny warbled. "It was a lightning fire."

"And?" Mr. Black asked.

The boy and girl looked at each other, perplexed. Lee threw up his hands. "We never saw you two?"

"Correct answer," Major White said. "You can go."

"We need a ride back to Roswell. All four tires on my car are blown out."

"Rough night for you kids. Give us a few minutes."

Mr. Black made his way back to the cars and conversed with a small group of men who had been waiting. After a few minutes, Mr. Black returned to the young couple and the Major.

"We're set," Mr. Black said. "The Major and I will drive you home."

Thank goodness, Jenny whispered under her breath. She made herself a promise. This would be the last time she and Lee would go parking.

"What about my car?" Lee inquired.

"We'll have it towed," Major White said, slipping behind the wheel of a dark colored automobile with a white star on the door. Mr. Black held open the door for Jenny and Lee to slide into the back seat. He joined the major in the front. After ascertaining Jenny's address, the major steered the car down the bumpy dirt road and then turned onto the highway back to town.

When the lights from Roswell finally came into view, Jenny squeezed Lee's hand, relieved that they were almost home.

The drive back to town had taken place in complete silence. Suddenly Lee asked, "What were those creatures? There were two creatures in the woods. We saw them."

Major White braked suddenly, turned the car about, and sped off in a different direction.

CHAPTER 3
Roswell via Las Vegas

Las Vegas, Nevada
July 7, 1947

The invitation arrived at 221B by special courier. The correspondence had originated in Washington, was passed along to Whitehall, and then to Holmes. After quickly consuming the contents of the letter marked *eyes only*, Holmes passed the document to me.

"Read it and burn it." He said, filling a pipe.

I quickly scanned the letter, then using the match Holmes had lit his pipe with, I set the letter ablaze and dropped it into the fireplace.

"Thoughts?" Holmes asked, drawing mightily on his pipe.

"The Americans have a high-profile murder involving a senator and a lady of the evening. It seems clear cut. Why involve you?"

"Clearly, the evidence is pointing in a direction that does not comport with the narrative the Americans wish to convey."

"Surely they can recast the crime scene however they wish."

"Unless others have already seen it and can offer a countervailing scenario of the events that unfolded."

"In other words, they need a credible and entirely disinterested third party. And who better to fit that bill than Sherlock Holmes?"

"Watson, really, you make me blush," Holmes chuckled.

"It really isn't our sort of thing, is it?"

"Not our sort of thing at all."

"Yet you intend to accept the case."

"You have gathered that, have you?"

"Holmes, we have been companions far too long. I should prove unworthy of your society if I failed to observe the expressions and mannerisms you exhibit when your intention is to accept a case."

"My expressions and mannerisms? Interesting. We shall pursue that notion at a future date. As I have no interest in a transatlantic crossing, I should normally decline such a case, especially since the purpose is to exploit my generous gifts. That this request comes from Whitehall, I must assume Mycroft owes the Americans a favor."

"It seems you have no choice."

"*We* have no choice, Watson. You will be joining me."

"Nothing in that letter remotely hinted at my involvement. You know very well I have a holiday planned."

"And you know very well I require your services."

"I know no such thing. My contributions to your solving of cases are all but negligible. You most certainly have no need of whatever it is you are attempting to coax me with."

We both knew I brought nothing to the table when it came to the unraveling of mysteries. My role was that of confidante and sounding board.

"Companionship, dear friend, companionship. It should go without saying, but I will say it anyway. I value your company as both a friend and colleague."

"Flattery, Holmes?"

"I abhor the idea."

"Sentiment then?"

"I am merely stating fact."

Fact indeed! Holmes could never allow such an admission. No matter. When it came to Holmes, I was a soft touch. We simply had too much history together for me to abandon him now. My holiday would wait.

Two days later we were on our way to the states via TWA Constellation.

The sensational murder case we had been called upon to help investigate had taken place in a suite of the recently opened Flamingo Hotel on the Las Vegas strip. Given the amount of time that had already passed, Holmes worried that critical evidence may have already been contaminated, possibly deliberately. For him, crime scene evidence was a living organism. It required care and nurture. He had seen too many flatfoots destroy evidence through carelessness. Cases had gone unsolved. Evidence had simply been allowed to perish.

Upon our arrival in Nevada, we were met at Alamo Field by Colonel Jim Patterson who filled us in on the details of the case as he knew them. He had flown in from Washington D.C. Those involved with the investigation had government security clearances, which meant local officials were to be kept out of the information loop. Cover stories were fabricated to conceal the sordid details from the public. It was all quite sensational and lurid, but in the end hardly worth our time.

According to Colonel Patterson, the senator had invited the young lady to his room for a cocktail. After several drinks, he became inebriated and abusive. When the young woman tried to lock herself in the bathroom, the senator kicked in the door. A bottle of cologne was knocked off the vanity and shattered on the bathroom tile. As he attempted to grab the young woman, the senator slipped on the spilt cologne, lost his footing and hit his head on the tile surrounding the shower stall. The blow to his head was fatal.

Without question, this senator of previously unblemished character had conducted himself in the most scandalous of ways. More to the point, the senator held a seat on a powerful senate committee of which his party currently held a one seat advantage. If the opposition could exploit the sordid details of the senator's murder, they might influence the choice of the deceased senator's replacement to turn the advantage in their favor. Could Holmes help?

"Now we are to it, Watson," Holmes whispered. "Politics, my friend, politics."

We were shown several photographs of the deceased senator and the fresh crime scene itself. Holmes spent very little time with the photos. He carefully studied the room and the bathroom in which the senator's fatal fall had presumably occurred. The carpet in the room designated as the living area was of special interest.

Accustomed as I was to the methods employed by Holmes, Colonel Patterson seemed anxious and felt the need to add to his previous narrative. Holmes raised his hand for silence.

"The senator did not die from a fall in the shower. He was killed earlier. His body was dragged into the bathroom. Note the lines in the carpet." Holmes pointed to the furrows in the carpet's pile. "A haphazard attempt has been made to smooth out the carpet. Perhaps with a Hoover. As to the smear on the tile surrounding the shower, it is far too bloody to have been produced by slipping and striking one's head. The bloody smear was applied post mortem."

"What about the scuff mark on the bathroom floor?" Colonel Patterson asked.

"Did you inspect the heels of the senator's shoes?"
"No."

"Observe." Holmes knelt. "Note this small gap in the scuff mark on the tile. This suggests a gouge in the heel of the shoe. An examination of the senator's shoes will reveal no such gap. Judging from the photographs in which the senator's shoes are clearly visible, the scuff mark is inconsistent with a man of the senator's weight. This mark was made with another shoe, one much lighter than the heavy wing tips worn by the senator. A heavier shoe would have produced a thicker layer of graphite. This mark is much too light."

"What about the murder weapon?"

"A champagne bottle."

"Champagne bottle? There was no champagne bottle."

"And yet there are two empty champagne glasses on the cocktail table. Judging by the nose of the empty glasses, a Dom Perignon '43. If you search the mezzanine two floors below this room, I suspect you will find the remains of a shattered champagne bottle. It is unlikely to have survived being dropped from the window."

Colonel Patterson snapped his fingers, immediately dispatching two officers to search the area below the senator's room.

"What about the cigar ash crushed into the carpet? The senator was a cigar smoker."

"The ash isn't that of a cigar. It is cigarette ash of a type of tobacco found in a dozen American cigarette brands. The ash, however, is irrelevant. It tells us only that someone smoked. Perhaps all three."

"Three?"

"Yes, the young woman and her accomplice."

"An accomplice? There is no indication of a third person."

"A hotel employee. A porter most likely."

"If this is the crime you believe it to be, what was the motive?"

"Extortion."

"How may we prove that?"

"Find the porter with the shoe that matches the mark on the bathroom floor. Review hotel records for the purchase of the champagne. Locate the camera among the porter's personal possessions."

"Mr. Holmes, are you certain?"

"Certainty is for the gods. Play the girl off against the accomplice with the gouge in his heel and you will have your answer."

"But the camera. How do you know a camera was involved?"

"Tiny slivers of glass in the pile of the carpet, consistent with that of a flash bulb. Too small to be easily vacuumed up. A porter would have easy access to a Hoover. The accomplice with the flash camera caught the senator with the young woman *In flagrante delicto* and threatened blackmail. When the senator resisted, he was killed. As the plot to blackmail the senator failed, the scene was staged to make it appear the young woman was an innocent victim."

Holmes turned his attention to me.

"Come Watson, let us try our luck in the casino. I am sure that calculating the odds of a jackpot will prove far more of a challenge than solving this crime has been."

Later that evening Holmes and I boarded a military plane with Colonel Patterson for Dulles Airport in Washington D.C. From there we were scheduled to board another transatlantic fight for London. Shortly after lifting off from Las Vegas, Colonel Patterson received a message from Army Air Forces Intelligence.

"My apologies, gentleman, but this flight has been ordered to divert to Roswell, New Mexico. H.Q. assures me they will be able to make alternate arrangements for your travel once we touch down at Roswell Army Air Field."

Half an hour later our plane landed in Roswell, New Mexico. Holmes and I exited the aircraft. We were led to a ready room. Colonel Patterson joined two other men in an adjoining room. The men were easily visible through the windows separating the two rooms. Colonel Patterson appeared to be listening attentively while the other two men engaged in an animated narrative, the content of which was impossible to discern. Periodically glances were directed toward Holmes and me and then the conversation resumed with much shaking and nodding of heads. As we were anxious to resume our journey back to London, whatever was taking place seemed to require an inordinate amount of discussion. Holmes had little patience for standing and doing nothing. At last some sort of resolution was reached and the two men exited. Colonel Patterson stood alone for a moment massaging a spot between his eyebrows, and then he rejoined Holmes and me in the ready room.

"I am afraid we have a situation."

"We gathered as much," Holmes said dismissively.

"It's all hush-hush, top-secret, if you know what I mean."

"Yes," I said quickly, wishing to forestall Holmes giving voice to his feelings. "We are familiar with that sort of thing, Colonel. We have consulted on numerous cases of utmost secrecy."

"It seems some sort of craft has crashed about seventy-five miles from here."

"A craft? What kind of craft? A plane. A helicopter? What?" Holmes asked.

"I can't be sure. There's a great deal of conflicting information. Possibly some casualties."

"Any eyewitnesses?" I asked.

"Possibly," the Colonel replied.

"How long ago?" Holmes inquired.

"At least two hours. It will take us at least an hour to arrive on scene."

"Us?" Holmes inquired.

"Yes, a helicopter is being readied for us now. I regret the inconvenience, but the brass thought you might be of use." The Colonel thought better of his word choice and changed *use* to *help*.

"We'll miss our flight to Washington," I protested.

"Sorry, Dr. Watson, you have already missed your flight."

I glanced at my watch. "We depart in six hours."

"Not tonight, Doctor. All outbound flights have been cancelled for the next several hours."

"Very well," Holmes demurred. "It seems we have no choice."

"I hoped you'd see it that way, Mr. Holmes."

An hour later the helicopter we had boarded circled the crash site, which was now little more than an orange glow of dying embers. Occasionally the flash of a camera would appear as lightning. Military personnel and vehicles were scattered about the perimeter of the crash site. A red warning light blinked to inform us that we were landing. On the ground makeshift landing lights outlined a temporary landing spot. A man with flags waved us in.

"Remain with me," the Colonel said, as we exited the helicopter. "Don't ask questions and don't touch anything."

"We know how to conduct ourselves, Colonel," Holmes said.

"Sorry to be so blunt. This is a highly classified area. The guards you see posted all around are carrying live ammunition."

Holmes and I followed Colonel Patterson to the smoldering remains of the object that had crashed.

Whatever the object had been was essentially disintegrated. Scattered about the scene was a fair amount of twisted metal, which looked to me like thin sheets of aluminium, or as the Americans say, aluminum.

"Wait here," the Colonel ordered. "I need to speak with those officers over there." He pointed to a group of men standing several yards away.

"Is it alright if I smoke," Holmes asked, pulling his pipe from his pocket.

"Fine, just don't touch anything."

"Thank you," Holmes said, turning abruptly and stumbling into me with such force that the collision of our bodies knocked his pipe to the ground.

"Good lord, Holmes, you almost knocked me over."

"Sorry, old chap." Holmes bent down to retrieve his pipe. "I must have rolled my foot on a branch." He slipped his pipe back into his coat pocket.

"I thought you were having a pipe."

"Couldn't find my matches."

"I have matches."

"Change of mind."

A quarter of an hour later Holmes and I had yet to be brought in on the matter. From our position well away from the men who had gathered in a small circle to assess the scene, we did manage to catch the odd word and phrase here and there of increasingly angry voices. "What the hell!" "The press!" "Orders!" "Damn it!" "Security!" "Head on a platter!"

"Holmes, I'm not sure why we were brought along. Not much good we're doing. What do you think is going on?"

Holmes shook his head. "Hard to say, old boy."

"Complete waste of time, if you ask me."

The angry voices subsided and turned to whispers as the small group of military men drew closer together. Heads nodded as if to indicate a consensus had been reached. The group broke apart and Colonel Patterson returned to the spot where Holmes and I were standing. "Sorry for keeping you waiting, false alarm."

"False alarm?" I said, barely able to conceal my surprise.

"Yes, Doctor, there's been some confusion."

"How so?" Holmes asked.

"Some misinformation made its way to the press. It turns out this is a big misunderstanding. This is not what it seems."

"Then what is it?" Holmes asked pointedly.

"Well, that is--" Colonel Patterson began, seemingly at a loss for words. "At the moment I am not at liberty to share any more information. An official statement will be issued."

"Then our services will not be required," Holmes replied.

"I am sure you and Dr. Watson would like to be on your way."

"Yes, we've had rather a long day," I said.

"Again, my apologies for the inconvenience. We'll have you back in Roswell as soon as possible."

A myriad of scheduling issues delayed Holmes and me an additional day. Instead of departing for Washington, Holmes and I would now be leaving from New York. We overnighted in Roswell and then flew nonstop the next day by military transport to a base near New York City. From there we were driven to La Guardia to await our long flight home to London. While awaiting our flight, I availed myself of several complimentary newspapers, each carrying the remarkable story of the incident we had been witness to two nights previously.

According to one account, the Army Air Forces were in possession of a flying saucer that had crashed onto a ranch in New Mexico.

"Flying saucer, indeed," I chuckled to myself.

Upon our return home, we discovered the papers in London had also devoted a fair amount of coverage to the Roswell story. As I had been at the scene of the crash, I paid little attention. I was too immersed in my writing to allow myself to become distracted.

CHAPTER 4
Dreams take flight

Kapustin Yar, Soviet Union
July 9, 1947

As a young boy living in the small village of Yaniv, some sixty miles from Kiev, Dmitri Sokolov determined early on to make more of his life than his parents had made of theirs. Dmitri's parents were poor, but not destitute. They managed to eke out a living farming and selling produce at the local market. At age seven Dmitri was expected to work the farm and then help transport the goods to market. Unlike most children in the village who had little formal education, Dmitri could read and write, thanks to an uncle who taught in Kiev. Whenever Dmitri visited his Uncle Maxim, Maxim always made sure Dmitri returned home with a book in hand. With little in the way of prospects, reading ignited Dmitri's imagination and dreams of success. At age seven perhaps he was naïve and unrealistic, yet he believed something better awaited. How his dreams would materialize he could not foresee. Then on a weekend visit to Kiev to celebrate his birthday, Dmitri's future unfolded before his eyes. The date was August 27, 1913.

"I take you someplace special," Uncle Maxim said.

"Tell me," Dmitri begged.

"You'll see. Is surprise."

Dmitri and his uncle boarded a bus for Syretzk Aerodrome located on the outskirts of Kiev. Upon arriving at the aerodrome young Dmitri's face lit up. He had never seen airplanes up close before. He had only ever seen them fly over his tiny village on occasion. Dmitri and his uncle joined a crowd of spectators that had gathered.

"It is wonderful, Uncle, so many airplanes. But why are all these people here?"

"You have heard of Pyotr Nesterov?"

Dmitri thought hard and shook his head.

"For shame," Uncle Maxim teased. "Pyotr Nesterov is the most famous pilot in all of Russia. You see that plane over there?" Uncle Maxim pointed to a plane standing apart from the others. "That plane is a special plane. It is a French Nieuport IV monoplane. They are flown by the best pilots of the Imperial Russian Air Service."

"Is Pyotr Nesterov going to fly that plane today?"

"Now you are catching on. Yes, that is why all these people are here today. Pyotr Nesterov is going to do something special."

"Is that he?" Dmitri cried out, pointing to a leather clad man walking toward the Nieuport IV."

"Yes," said Uncle Maxim.

"But what will he do?" Dmitri asked.

"You will see."

As Dmitri and his uncle moved to join other spectators seated in a makeshift grandstand, Pyotr Nesterov climbed into his plane and gave a thumbs-up to a crewman awaiting the signal to spin the prop. After a couple of spins and putts and smoke, the monoplane roared to life. With another thumbs-up for the benefit of the spectators Nesterov steered the plane onto the landing strip, powered up, and sped down the runway. Within seconds the plane lifted off. The spectators applauded. Nesterov made several passes over the aerodrome.

"Is that it?" Dmitri asked.

"Watch," Uncle Maxim replied.

After flying level for several minutes, the Nieuport made an incredibly steep climb to an altitude of 1000 meters. The spectators gasped as the plane nosed almost straight up. The engine whined as if it could give no more power. And then the impossible happened. The plane pitched backwards, rolled upside down, and the engine stopped. Onlookers screamed. At least two people in the grandstand fainted. Something had gone terribly wrong. The plane was suddenly falling back to earth. Dmitri's heart jumped into his throat. He covered his eyes. He could not bear to watch as the plane rolled and tumbled back to earth. "Will he parachute to safety?" Someone screamed. "Jump, jump!" Others screamed. Tragedy appeared unavoidable. The plane tumbled for an unbearably long time. Then, impossibly, the Nieuport's engine came to life. The plane came out of its dive, leveled off, and Pyotr Nesterov landed safely and triumphantly in front of a stunned crowd. Pyotr Nesterov had just performed the first dead loop in aviation history.

The spectacular stunt made an immediate national hero of Nesterov, but not before he spent ten days under arrest for recklessly risking the destruction of government property.

From that day forward Dmitri knew what he wanted to do. Not only did he want to fly, he wanted to learn everything he could about aviation. That one could do such things with an airplane seemed impossible. How had Nesterov undertaken such a feat? Why hadn't the plane broken apart? He had to know and so he began reading everything about aviation he could get his hands on. Whenever he visited Uncle Maxim, a trip to the aerodrome was always expected. By the time Dmitri was old enough to enlist in the Soviet Air Force, he knew more about aviation than most of his instructors. Dmitri Sokolov rose quickly through the ranks and attained the rank of major general, something that impressed others more than he. Should it be necessary to address Sokolov by rank, he preferred major. He was a man of science and aviation; he did not consider himself a military man. The military had been a vehicle for obtaining an education.

Now, at age forty-four Dmitri Sokolov had succeeded far beyond his boyhood dreams. He had been named Director of Aviation Science and Technology. Through dogged determination and hard work Sokolov had been awarded the greatest gift of all. He was charged with overseeing a top-secret program at Kapustin Yar, a missile test range that had been developed under the supervision of Vasily Voznyuk to test and develop missile technology that had been appropriated from the Germans after the war. Sokolov's department was entirely separate from the missile program. It was housed in its own facility at the expansive Kapustin Yar missile launch site. As head of Science and Aviation Technology, Sokolov had an unlimited budget and a staff of the finest aviation scientists in the country to develop technologies that would propel the Soviet Union toward its goal of being first into space. That goal was years away, but Sokolov had little doubt his country would succeed.

As he stared at the bleak Russian landscape through his office window high above Kapustin Yar, Sokolov felt ambivalent about what he had achieved professionally thus far. He had accomplished much, yet one's value to the state was rarely judged by past accomplishments. More was always expected. Since the end of the war, his country's relationship with the West had soured. Suspicion and mistrust were apparent on both sides, particularly with the Americans. Yet to be fully realized by the citizens of either nation, a race in aviation and arms technology was well underway between the Soviets and the Americans. Hiroshima and Nagasaki had released the genie from the bottle. There was no turning back. Was this really the best of all possible worlds?

Sokolov's thoughts were interrupted by a knock at his office door.

"Come," said Sokolov.

Yuri Olenev, a trusted junior officer, entered.

"Major, we have received some interesting information from the U.S. It is in all of the newspapers."

"Go on," Sokolov said, continuing to stare through the window.

"Two days ago, there was an incident near Roswell, New Mexico. A flaming object streaked across the sky and then crashed to earth. It was witnessed by hundreds of citizens."

"A meteor, no doubt."

"According to the local newspaper, an eye witness claims it was a flying saucer. A spokesman for the intelligence agency housed at Roswell confirmed the story."

Sokolov turned to his aide. "U.S. intelligence is confirming a saucer crash?"

"Initially. The story has since been retracted. The official revised version now reports the object was a weather balloon. The individual who confirmed the original story was confused."

"Weather balloons do not streak across the sky."

"Apparently it exploded and burst into flames."

"Flaming weather balloons also do not streak across the sky. They fall from the sky."

"Washington's response is curious."

"What are you thinking, Yuri?"

"The Americans could easily pass this incident off as a meteor. That they did not suggests something did indeed crash. It would have been easy enough to deny."

"Why not deny?"

31

"Too many witnesses?"

"The question becomes, what are they concealing and why?"

"An experimental aircraft perhaps?"

"Possibly," Sokolov agreed. "There could be another possibility. The Americans may be further along on Project 1794 than we have been led to believe. If what crashed is a prototype that means the Americans are very close to succeeding with anti-gravity propulsion. It would make sense to create a cover story, no matter how implausible."

"I cannot think the Americans are that far along."

"Who is our agent in the region?"

"Cherepanov," Yuri said. "According to Director Shubin's office, he is fairly new. He was recruited by our operative for the Western Region."

"He is a Russian?"

"Most likely an American of Russian extraction. Foreign Intelligence has had little success placing native Russians in America. They tend not to adapt well. These days we rely mainly on sympathizers. I know nothing about this agent. Director Shubin shares little."

"Since Comrade Shubin was promoted to Director of Foreign Espionage, intelligence — I use that word loosely — has been a roll of the dice. The only thing Shubin did well was to chase women. The Kremlin should have left him where he was, stumbling around Europe playing the role of international spy." Sokolov waved a hand. "Enough of Shubin! How do we know we can trust this Cherepanov?"

"For no longer than he has been on the job, he sends his reports on time. He has yet to provide a lot of information; what he has provided seems accurate and authentic."

"Put Cherepanov to the test. I want to know more about this Roswell incident."

"Will there be anything else?"

Sokolov thought for a moment.

"If the crash in Roswell is a Project 1794 prototype, we need more detailed information than we have received so far from Shubin's mole. Get in touch with Shubin and make him aware of the Roswell incident, should he not know. Have him instruct his mole in Ohio to become more aggressive. At the pace we are currently proceeding, it will be the turn of the century before we have an operable saucer."

Yuri Olenev saluted and exited his superior's office.

CHAPTER 5
Eyewitness account

Roswell
July 11, 1947

The initial account of a spaceship crashing into a remote area of Chaves County first appeared in the *Roswell Daily Record* the day after the crash. The story was attributed to a local miner. In the early confusion of the incident an Army Air Forces official confirmed that the object that had crashed was indeed an alien ship and that pieces of the wrecked craft were in government possession. Shortly thereafter reinforcements arrived on scene, sealed off the area, and imposed a press blackout. Clarifications were issued and the following day a revised story appeared in the press debunking everything that had been previously reported. The object in question was not an alien spacecraft. It was in fact a high-altitude weather balloon that had exploded in the atmosphere and crashed back to Earth. As members of the public would not be familiar with such a weather-monitoring device, it was understandable how it could have been mistaken for something else. The crash area had been thoroughly investigated and cleaned up. Crews had worked tirelessly to restore the area to its previous condition.

No mention had been made of the unusual looking creatures. Abe Carl wasn't surprised. It seemed impossible that the swarm of government agents who first arrived would not have seen the creatures. No mention had been made for a reason. The government had something it wanted to keep quiet. Passing off the object as a weather balloon was proof of that. The story he had given to his friend at the newspaper had already been retracted and replaced with a lie. So be it. What he knew, he would keep to himself.

A few days later a story appeared about a pair of high school sweethearts gone missing. The last time anyone had seen them was the night of the crash. Earlier that afternoon they had driven from Roswell to Corona to visit the grandparents of the young man. The couple had left around six in the evening but never arrived home. Local authorities did not seem particularly concerned, as it was well known the couple had been dating for several years and most likely had run away from home to get married. No doubt they would soon turn up as happy newlyweds.

Abe Carl lingered over this new development for some time. He thought he might have seen two other people that night. Was the missing young couple the ones whose light he had seen before the cars arrived? He couldn't be sure. He had no way of proving what he saw. Officials had scrubbed the area clean. If the young couple had been out there that night, they would surely have been found.

A week later another newspaper known for running sensational stories interviewed Abe Carl to see if he had anything to add to his original story. The old miner was smarting over local gossip. In a few days he had gone from *Local Miner* to *Loco Miner*. What the hell! Abe Carl was only too happy to set the record straight. Let folks chew on this. The time had come to share the secret he had been keeping.

"I was in the mine when I felt the crash. I thought it was a tremor, so I figured I better hightail it out. In the distance, I could see flames. That's when I figured it was a fireball, you know, a meteorite. We see a lot of them out this way, but it wasn't that. It was a disc of some kind. Only it was on fire. I know what the guys in the black suits are saying, but it wasn't no weather balloon. I can guarantee you that. By the time I got close enough to it, it was pretty much engulfed in flames. And that's when I saw them. There was two of them. They was like nothing I ever seen before. They was green and lizard-like. They appeared shaken. When I shined my light on them, they took off. What happened to them after, I can't tell you. You should ask the feds, but my guess is you won't get a word out of them."

***

"Preposterous!" I tossed the newspaper I had just finished reading onto the side table in Holmes's apartment.

"What's that, old chap?" Holmes was studying an object on his desk with a magnifying glass.

"This newspaper account of that object in Roswell. I see now the cause of Colonel Patterson's consternation. It seems an eyewitness is claiming the object is some sort of alien spacecraft. A flying saucer, he calls it. He says he also saw lizard men. Absolute tommyrot. We were there. I saw no spacemen. I imagine it is exactly what the Americans say it is, a weather balloon that exploded and fell back to earth."

"Hmmm," said Holmes, clearly distracted.

"It is utterly ridiculous, don't you think, Holmes?"

Holmes picked up the object he had been studying under the magnifying glass and held it up to the light. "I'm not so sure, Watson."

"What? What's that then?" I asked, indicating the object Holmes was holding in his hand.

"It is a piece of material from the crash site. I retrieved it when I bent down to pick up my pipe."

"A piece of the weather balloon?"

"I don't think so, Watson." Holmes turned the pliable piece of metal in his hand. "I don't believe it was a weather balloon at all."

CHAPTER 6
Update

Kapustin Yar
July 15, 1947

The red light on Dmitri Sokolov's intercom blinked. "Yes, what is it?"

"We have received some additional information from America about the Roswell incident," Yuri Olenev replied. "As the Americans would say, the plot thickens."

"Bring it to me."

A moment later Yuri Olenev entered Sokolov's office with an attaché case and a tape recorder. He placed both items on his major's desk, stood at attention, and saluted.

Sokolov brushed off the salute. "Yuri, it isn't necessary to keep saluting me. There are no hidden cameras here. Now, what is this new information? Does it come from Cherepanov?"

"No, this information comes from a telephone intercept. It was passed along by Director Shubin's office. It is a recording of an American Army Air Forces colonel. His name is Patterson. He is married, but he has a mistress in Texas."

"Shubin's operatives have managed to bug the telephone of an American colonel?"

"The bug is on the telephone of the mistress. It is easy to tap the telephone of a hairdresser in a small Texas town. Tapping the telephone of a colonel on an American military base is impossible. Patterson uses a pay telephone when he calls. He is one of several officers we follow whose extracurricular activities make them vulnerable. At some future point the threat of exposure might prove useful. He and the woman speak once a week. Usually it is about nothing important." Yuri switched on the tape recorder. "Listen for yourself. I will play the relevant part, unless you want to hear all of it."

"No," Sokolov said.

The recording began with the woman laughing. Then she said, "You have been a very bad boy. Mommy will have to spank you when she sees you again."

Sokolov rolled his eyes.

Patterson spoke with a clear Texas accent. "You'll never guess who I met a couple of days ago."

"How would I know? Tell me!"

"Sherlock Holmes and Dr. Watson."

The woman laughed. "That English detective?"

"The one and only."

Sokolov raised his hand for Yuri to pause the recording. "Did I hear that correctly?"

"I thought you would be interested."

"Turn it back on."

The woman continued. "Go on, you didn't. Where did you meet Sherlock Holmes?"

"Roswell."

"Roswell? Was the King of England with him?"

"Charlene, I'm telling you, it's the truth."

"Did you get a picture?"

"No, it was official business. It wasn't the kind of thing where you could take pictures."

"So, what is he like?"

"He's okay. Not especially talkative. Dr. Watson you can talk to."

"How did you meet them?"

"I can't talk about that part."

"Hell, Jimmy, it doesn't take a genius. You said Roswell. Nobody ever heard of that place until that flying saucer crashed. Is that what it was about?"

"Charlene, it wasn't a saucer. It was a weather balloon."

"Jimmy, I may be just a simple hairdresser, but nobody believes that story. The old man who said he saw space aliens, he's the one everyone believes."

Sokolov signaled for Yuri to pause the tape.

"What is she talking about?"

"We're getting to that."

The tape resumed.

"That old man, he's just an old drunk."

"Everyone who comes into the shop believes him."

"Forget that nonsense," Patterson said, quickly changing the subject." I got you a present."

"You did? Tell me, what did you get me?"

Yuri switched off the tape recording.

"Should you be wondering, the gift was lingerie."

"Of course. The only thing men buy women is something for themselves."

Yuri couldn't help but chuckle. Sokolov was the only senior officer with a sense of humor.

Sokolov lit a custom blended cigarette. "This weather balloon story that even a simple hairdresser does not believe is beginning to look very suspicious. If it were nothing, why would the Americans bring in Sherlock Holmes? On the other hand, if the crash was the 1794 prototype, we may ask ourselves the same question. What can Holmes tell the Americans they cannot discover for themselves?"

"That remains to be seen."

"What is this business about an old man?"

"Here is where the story gets very interesting. She is speaking about the miner who first reported the incident. He has amended his story."

"Retracted, you mean?" Sokolov said.

"Amended. He now claims to have seen two alien beings that night. As you may well imagine, this story has taken on a life of its own. One might pass the story off as the ravings of a lunatic, but there may also be other witnesses."

Yuri pulled a copy of an American newspaper from his attaché case. Next to a follow up story of the Roswell crash was a photograph of a young couple.

"This boy and this girl may have been at the scene that night. The boy's car was found incinerated. The couple has yet to be found. They are listed as officially missing."

"Presumed dead?"

"Possibly."

"Is there a reason to doubt that conclusion?"

"The miner believes he may have seen the couple alive that night."

"The same miner who believes he may have seen space aliens?"

"To be sure, he has little credibility. But what if he did see what he reported? What if the missing couple is alive? Might they not be in protective custody? If so, what had they seen that the Americans wish to keep secret?"

Sokolov thought for a moment. "By keeping the boy and girl hidden, there is no one to corroborate the miner's story."

"Correct," Yuri said.

"But we do not know if the boy and girl are alive." Sokolov said.

"Bringing Holmes and Watson to the crash scene suggests there is more to this story than a weather balloon covering up an ordinary crash. The Americans are trying to keep something secret."

"If the young couple is still alive, then they and Holmes and Watson become invaluable assets."

"Major, is it possible the Americans really have captured an alien spacecraft?"

"Yuri, there is not a shred of evidence that these sightings seen the world over are alien craft."

"I agree Major. It borders on fantasy. But we cannot prove they are not. For the sake of argument, what if the Americans really are in possession of an alien craft and its crew?"

"Then for the Soviet Union, the space race is effectively over."

CHAPTER 7
Dugway

Utah, 1950

Lt. Wes Reed followed in the footsteps of his father. The elder Reed had been a pilot during the First World War, and he himself served as a pilot during World War II. When the war came to an end, Reed remained with the Army Air Forces until September of 1947 when the Air Force was reorganized as a separate branch of the U.S. defense program. Reed's passion was to fly. Any commercial airline company would have hired him in an instant, but for Wes Reed flying was a thrill; he liked the danger. In the Air Force one was able to fly lots of different craft. Over the years Reed had proved his prowess in all manner of planes. He was known as Air Ace 1. He was widely regarded as the best of the best, an appellation he not only enjoyed, but attempted to cultivate as well. As Air Ace 1, Reed usually received first crack at the latest experimental aircraft that found their way to the Dugway Proving Ground in Utah. For a time, Reed was the proverbial golden boy, and then his career derailed.

During a test flight of a new experimental fighter, Reed pushed the aircraft beyond its limits, causing the fighter to stall. His only option was to eject, which resulted in the destruction of the aircraft. A formal inquiry found Reed had ignored protocols and suspended him from flying for six months.

Few among the public knew of Dugway. It had been established in secret during the early forties for the development and testing of chemical weapons. Located 13 miles south of the Utah Test and Training Range, a fair number of experimental aircraft that had been tested at

The Range were now housed in secret facilities at Dugway, which helped explain the unusually high number of UFO sightings in the Western United States.

Among the secret aircraft stationed at Dugway was the FD3, the third in a series of flying discs that had been developed by the top-secret Chimera division of the Air Force. The FD3 was the culmination of years of research that began under the name Project 1794. Project 1794 began in Hangar 18 at Wright-Patterson. In preparation for test flights, the FD3 was disassembled and moved in pieces to Dugway.

At age 32, Lt. Wes Reed and fellow pilot Mark Daniels had been named as the official test pilots of the FD3. For Reed the assignment was a bitter disappointment.

The FD3 was a huge, cumbersome ship fraught with problems. Resigning his commission to take a position with a private firm was not an option; his six months suspension had seen to that.

Development of the FD3 was a long and difficult process. The ship had proved far more challenging than conventional aircraft that relied on jet propulsion. The original design for an anti-gravity propulsion power source was scrapped early on. In theory the anti-gravity propulsion system should work; the reality was the technology had yet to catch up with theory. In its place a gravitational electromagnetic system was developed. Known as the GEM, the new propulsion system was promising. The full extent of its range had yet to be determined. The first successful flight had occurred two years earlier. Immediately the Air Force hailed the FD as a success and insisted it be rushed into production. Engineers working on the project did not share that enthusiasm. Caution was warranted. There were still many issues to resolve. Primary among those issues was the concern that the higher the craft flew, the less effective the propulsion became. Determining a maximum range for the FD3 was not yet possible. Test flights were of limited range at pre-set altitudes.

Wes Reed and Mark Daniels both believed the FD3 was capable of a range well beyond the limits imposed by the Dugway engineers, but their arguments fell on deaf ears. Given his history, Reed knew not to press the matter.

During that two-year period of test flights, Reed and Daniels were limited to flying at night. The tests required landings and take offs, acceleration tests, and maneuverability tests. Landings took place in remote locations, well away from population centers. The routines had become so familiar, both pilots felt they could do their jobs in their sleep. Both the thrill and the challenge of flying had long since passed.

For Reed, a pilot addicted to speed and danger, he missed the adventure of the old days. Unlike the supersonic fighters he had previously tested, the FD3 had all the appeal of a fully loaded cargo plane.

The Chimera program was shrouded in secrecy. Yet there were those locals who inhabited the remote areas within the FD3's regular flight path that knew of the secret aircraft. Every few weeks one could count on a saucer sighting. In the beginning the Air Force received a few citizen inquiries. The excuses and denials were always the same: balloons, clouds, gas formations, and natural phenomena, among other explanations. Eventually the calls tapered off. No one bothered to report the sightings. Nothing had ever come of the Roswell incident. No one ever came to investigate. Why bother?

Reed and Daniels sat in the ready room smoking and drinking coffee. The FD3 was being moved into position and readied for that night's flight. Launch was still twenty minutes away. Reed lit a cigarette and unsealed the flight plan envelope. He quickly glanced over the details of the evening's flight and passed the document to Daniels.

"When do we get to see what this pie plate can really do?" Daniels asked. "I am tired of all these short hops."

Reed shrugged. "No use talking to the guys in engineering. All I get from them is 'We're working on it.' I've told them until I am blue in the face this thing can do more. What do I know? I'm the guy who crashed a jet worth a million dollars."

"It could be worse," Daniels said.

"Maybe. I could have been assigned a desk job."

"I'm talking about the Soviets."

"What do you mean by that? What about the Soviets?"

Daniels glanced around and lowered his voice. "Just between you and me. Okay?"

Reed rolled his eyes. Daniels was about to go into one of his long and boring stories.

"I was in this bar. It must have been six or seven months ago. These two guys from propulsion were there, in the next booth, knocking down drink after drink, talking too loudly. One tells the other that the boys at the top discovered a mole in the Project 1794 program at Wright-Patterson. He'd been smuggling plans out of the country for some time. Which makes sense, now that we know the Soviets have their own saucer project. Anyway, someone in Chimera caught on, but instead of exposing the mole, they started feeding him the plans to the AGP system."

"A propulsion system that doesn't work," Reed said.

"Exactly! Here's the beauty of it all. They did it in such a way that the Soviets won't make that discovery until the ship is almost operational. The Soviets have spent years developing an FD3 clone that isn't going to fly. Pretty smart."

Reed stubbed out his cigarette. "Very."

"That gives you something to think about."

Reed nodded thoughtfully.

"What I'd give to be there when the Russians find out," Daniels said. "Oh, boy! Heads are going to roll."

Thirty minutes later the FD3 took off for its routine run over the dark Utah terrain. The elliptical flight path would take the ship over the tip of eastern Arizona, western New Mexico, through Colorado, Nebraska, western South Dakota, and Wyoming before returning to Dugway. Each flight mission required Reed to land the saucer at a pre-determined location and wait fifteen minutes, at which point Daniels would take over as pilot. After returning to Dugway, the ship would be carefully gone over for signs of structural fatigue and mechanical issues. Both Reed and Daniels knew the ship was airworthy. A craft as sophisticated as the FD3 ought to be able to outperform the Air Force's fastest jet. Given the chance, they'd show the boys in engineering what the FD3 could do.

CHAPTER 8
The Olympus Project

Kapustin Yar, 1950

The giant hangar at Kapustin Yar bore no markings. There were no numbers and no letters to identify the imposing structure. It was known simply as The Hangar. It was one of many structures at the secret Soviet facility. Throughout the sprawling complex designers, machinists, and technicians worked at developing top-secret aircraft to meet the challenges of a post-war Soviet Union. For the members of the group known as The Team, Kapustin Yar was a magic box filled with unlimited possibilities. With no limits on budget and no restrictions on what could be designed, The Team had been given free rein to make their dreams come true. Inside The Hangar was the most ambitious project ever undertaken in Soviet aviation. Known by its codename TOP, the acronym stood for The Olympus Project.

Dmitri Sokolov pushed through the door within the giant pair of sliding doors that allowed a craft to move in and out of The Hangar. He switched on the lights. The hangar lit up as bright as day. In the center of the mammoth building stood a gleaming silver flying saucer.

From the beginning TOP had its critics. Jet propulsion was still in its infancy. Why was Sokolov developing something so radical and so advanced? Sokolov had a simple reply. "Because the Americans are. We are building a ship from their plans."

For years technicians had been busily working from detailed plans smuggled from the United States to build a Soviet version of America's Project 1794.

"As much as the Americans would like to believe they will be the undisputed aerospace leaders in the world, we shall be their equals," Sokolov reminded his doubters of the success the Germans had had with the V-1 and V-2 rockets.

The doubters reminded Sokolov of what had befallen Germany. Untold millions had been spent on this folly. The new anti-gravity propulsion system was untested. Sokolov resisted. Development would continue.

Sokolov went upstairs to the office that overlooked the giant hangar. He had engaged in this ritual every night for a week, poring over the plans for the anti-gravity propulsion system. Each night he came to the same inescapable conclusion.

Since first learning of the Roswell incident, the once steady stream of stolen Project 1794 plans had been reduced to a trickle. Despite Sokolov's demand for more, the mole in Ohio could not risk discovery. The Olympus Project was advancing, but much too slowly. Meanwhile, intelligence had confirmed the Americans were routinely engaged in test flights with a saucer referred to as the FD3. So far it had only been capable of short distance low altitude flights. Sokolov knew it was only a matter of time before the Americans would have formidable capabilities. And then there was always the lingering question of Roswell. Yet those concerns paled in comparison to what he had recently discovered.

While attending an international air show in Europe, Sokolov had been approached by a French woman who claimed to have important information regarding The Olympus Project.

"What is The Olympus Project?" Sokolov asked. "I have never heard of it."

The woman handed Sokolov a large envelope. "I am only a courier, Major."

Without opening the envelope, Sokolov asked, "What does the sender want in return?"

"It is a sign of good faith. The sender may need your help one day in obtaining Soviet citizenship. Good day, Major." The woman quickly disappeared into the crowd.

It wasn't until he returned to his hotel room later that evening that Sokolov made his discovery. Upon his return home, Sokolov began his nightly vigil poring over the blueprints for TOP until he was convinced beyond a certainty that the information he had been given was one hundred percent accurate.

Sokolov invited Yuri Olenev to the giant hangar. It was a bitterly cold night. The team of workers had retired for the day, having returned to their dormitories to relax and socialize until they reported to work again the next morning. Sokolov's crew was diligent, meticulously following the stolen American blueprints. Although the pace of construction had slowed, everyone working on the project was optimistic that the saucer was only months away from launch. As the project neared completion, the naysayers in the Kremlin began to change their tune. The Soviet Union was about to show the world what it was capable of, and the U.S. would be humiliated that the plans to their top-secret program had been stolen.

Sokolov shook his head and pushed his hands through his hair. "I have gone over these plans a thousand times, Yuri. It is inescapable. TOP will never fly."

Tears welled up in the young officer's eyes. "It is ninety percent complete. How could this have happened?"

"There can be only one explanation. The Americans discovered our mole. He was tricked into sending flawed blueprints. Who knows how long?"

"Why didn't we see this? How could we have known?" Yuri asked.

"When the delivery of plans slowed to a trickle, that should have told us something. Not only did they manage to slow down our development by sending us fewer documents, it made seeing the whole picture more difficult. This was played beautifully, Yuri. Not only are we behind, we have a white elephant on our hands. We will be crucified, if not executed."

"Major, I am at a loss. What do we do? How do we proceed?"

"For the foreseeable future, we will rely on that well-tested Soviet axiom, waste as much time as you can."

During the weeks that followed, Yuri Olenev was a nervous wreck. His fellow officers asked if Yuri were well. Lately he looked tired, his features were drawn. Yuri assured his colleagues he was well. It was nothing more than a few nights of fitful sleep.

Sokolov also noticed how stressed his young assistant was. He offered reassurances. "We have to hold up, Yuri."

"I am sorry Major. I feel as if the sword of Damocles is hanging above our heads. The thread is fraying. Any moment this may all come crashing down. I am completely beside myself. How do we make this go away?"

"We come up with a plan," Sokolov said.

"A plan?" Yuri asked incredulously. "What kind of plan?"

"A plan that makes heroes of us. The Americans have made fools of us. We make fools of them."

Yuri laughed nervously. "In all due respect Major, I can only think of one scenario, and that borders on insanity."

Sokolov slapped Yuri on the back. "And that, Yuri, is the plan we shall prepare for. We shall call it Operation Dead Loop. It will be our plan of last resort. We will succeed brilliantly, or we shall fail spectacularly. We have no choice Yuri. If we have any hope of survival, we must begin moving the pieces on the chessboard."

Yuri left his superior's office convinced the Major was mentally unhinged.

CHAPTER 9
Double exposure

Moscow, 1951

Morning in Moscow was unusually sunny and warm. Tatiana Andreyev was glad. She took advantage of the fresh, warm air, drinking in as much as possible on her walk to work before pushing through the large iron gates of the Lubyanka Building, where she worked as a photographic analyst. Once inside there would be no hint of the beautiful day beyond the walls. There were no windows where she worked. Her department was below ground, where there was nothing but rows of desks, flickering fluorescent lights, and piles of American newspapers to pore through. Such was the work of a low-level analyst. Her job was classified, which meant she could never tell her girlfriends what she did. Her friends believed her to be an insurance underwriter. They could never understand why she couldn't underwrite insurance policies for them. Her excuse was never mix business and friends.

Tatiana's job was part of the Soviet Union's vast intelligence network. She and the five other young women who shared the same cubicle were tasked with studying photographs in American newspapers. On its surface the job seemed better suited for a simpleton. It was anything but that. The job required a photographic memory, which was always the standard joke among her fellow analysts. One needed a photographic memory to analyze photographs. What precisely were these analysts looking for? They were looking for anything and everything. Who was in the news? Why? Did a current photograph relate to a past photograph? Were there images in the backgrounds that warranted a closer look?

As Tatiana's supervisor reminded her and her clutch of analysts more than once, *there is more than meets the eye than meets the eye.* In other words, at first glance a photograph does not reveal its secrets. Tatiana did not believe photographs held secrets, only that they revealed more information the closer you looked. By the time lunch rolled around, Tatiana had scanned more than one hundred newspapers. The morning had produced nothing of note. Although Tatiana was diligent in her duties, she often found herself dreaming about the lives of those she saw in the photographs and thought how nice it would be to live in America. During the noon break, she and her friends took their lunch outside. Fresh air cleared the mind and the eyes. Since talk about the job was forbidden, lunchtime conversation always turned to gossip or relationships. Thirty minutes was never enough time to get everything in, but one knew never to complain, especially if one wished to advance. The whistle blew. Lunch was over.

"Back to the salt mines," someone said. This was another joke enjoyed by all. Lunchtime never passed without someone speaking those words.

An hour into her afternoon shift, Tatiana was turning through the pages of the Wright-Patterson daily newspaper. It was the official newspaper of an American air base located in Dayton, Ohio. Tatiana took delight in comparing the fashions of American women to those of Soviet women. The women in America were far more stylish, she thought. It was in crowd photos such as the one she was looking at that she got most of her own fashion ideas. The photograph that had drawn her attention was that of a Fourth of July celebration. She presumed the crowd of onlookers in the photograph was watching a parade. As she scanned the photograph, one image gave her pause. It was of an attractive fair-haired young woman cupping her hands over her eyes to shield herself from the glare of the sun. The face seemed familiar. Tatiana's photographic memory began its search of files. As she sorted her memory file, an image of a young woman with her arms folded in front of her began to form. When and where had she seen that image? The current photo was taken near an air base. What about the previous photo? Could it also have something to do with an air base? No. Was it something about aviation? Perhaps. As she dug deeper into her memory banks, the word Roswell came to mind. She went to the bank of filing cabinets arranged alphabetically and opened a drawer in the R section. After several minutes she came across a copy of the *Roswell Daily Record*. A few days after the UFO crash in 1947, a photograph of a missing teenage couple appeared. Tatiana pulled the newspaper from the file and compared the picture of the missing girl with the picture of the girl in the crowd. The photographs were taken at least four years apart. Clearly there were obvious differences. But more features were alike than different. Whatever doubt Tatiana Andreyev may have entertained was put to rest with the ring that was clearly visible in both photographs. To be certain, Tatiana invited her cubicle companions to view the two photographs. Immediately the other girls focused on the photograph of the missing boy and started giggling. After a gentle admonishment, the girls arrived at a unanimous verdict. There was no doubt both photographs were of the same young woman. Encouraged by the certainty of her fellow analysts, Tatiana presented both photographs to her supervisor.

After a cursory inspection, the supervisor said, "Well done, Comrade. Your good work will be noted and rewarded."

Tatiana should have been pleased by her supervisor's praise, but nothing had ever come of past praise and promises of reward. "One more to add to the list," Tatiana said to herself. She watched as her supervisor took the stairs to the floor above.

Tatiana's supervisor presented herself and her diligent hard work to her own supervisor; she never bothered to mention Tatiana Andreyev had done the work.

Ever since word of the Roswell case in America had reached the Soviet Union, all intelligence agencies had been put on notice that anything concerning Roswell was to be immediately forwarded to Major Sokolov. By the end of the day both photographs were sealed in an envelope, marked *eyes only*, and sent by courier to Kapustin Yar.

CHAPTER 10
The Photograph

Kapustin Yar

Dmitri Sokolov carefully studied the two photographs Director Shubin's office had forwarded to him from Moscow. There were differences indeed between the two images of the young woman, but as had been pointed out by others, a young woman will change over a period of years. It was the ring, however, that left no doubt. Its design was unique. And now this girl who reportedly died or disappeared the night of the Roswell crash site suddenly appears in a crowd near Wright-Patterson Air Force Base. Hardly a coincidence, Sokolov thought. It was common knowledge within Soviet Intelligence that Wright-Patterson housed a secret facility on base referred to as Hangar 18. It was there the Americans had developed Project 1794. As he and Yuri had speculated in the days after the Roswell incident was reported, the Americans had something to hide. Unconfirmed reports also suggested whatever had been found at the Roswell crash site had been transferred to Hangar 18. Four years later this missing girl turns up near a base known for the development of advanced aviation technology. Coincidence? Perhaps. From the start, the Roswell incident left too many questions unanswered. There were too many unknowns. Now what to make of a photograph, and in a military publication for that matter? Were the Americans really that careless? Surely, they were smarter than that. "We shall see," Sokolov said to himself. The truth may be elusive, but he would find it. Four years after the Roswell incident, Cherepanov had provided nothing useful beyond that which appeared in newspapers. In addition to feeding the

Soviets worthless plans, the Americans had done a masterful job of keeping a lid on Roswell.

The climate in the Kremlin had changed. The optimism expressed when it was believed The Olympus Project was only months away from completion had now evaporated. Concerns from the Kremlin were growing ever louder. The Cold War with the West was consuming unprecedented resources and money. Officials were becoming impatient with Sokolov. They had tired of his reminders that advanced technologies required time. That it could be another year yet was out of the question. The threat of a visit any day didn't particularly concern Sokolov. Kapustin Yar was too remote, and officials who might visit would have about as much technological knowledge as a worm.

One of Sokolov's tactics for delay involved having his crew of technicians disassemble parts of the ship under the guise of quality control concerns. Such orders made no difference to his technicians. To them a job was a job. They were inside and warm. For Sokolov and Yuri Olenev, the thread holding that sword of above their heads could unravel at any moment.

Yuri Olenev was all too aware of the increasing unrest in Moscow. More and more he was feeling as if he were a caged animal. Something had to give. As a good Soviet he could simply betray Sokolov and pretend ignorance, but everyone knew he and Sokolov were joined at the hip. Whatever fate might befall Major Sokolov would also befall him.

"Has the time come to implement Operation Dead Loop?" Yuri asked.

Sokolov studied the photograph of the young girl. "We are not yet standing on the edge of the abyss. This girl could be of value to us. If she really is the one who disappeared shortly after the Roswell crash, she may have information that might earn us the goodwill of those clowns in Moscow. I think we must plan an operation to find out what she knows."

"She is hardly out of her teens. What could she know?"

"She knows something about Roswell. There can be no other explanation for her disappearance. Assemble a team and plan an operation to locate this young woman. I want to know once and for all what happened at Roswell. There are those who believe the Americans have an alien ship in their possession. I never believed in that conspiracy nonsense. I have always believed the crash was a Project 1794 prototype. Our knowledge of their secret programs is no secret. They have been feeding us worthless plans for years. So why continue to shroud Roswell in mystery? There has always been something more to this. We have always been convinced of that. What this girl knows may be the only way to turn down the heat on us. The time has come to find out."

"Major, we are risking our reputations, perhaps our lives, on a young woman whom we cannot be sure knows anything."

"I think that is a chance we must take. Otherwise we have no choice but to turn on each other."

Sokolov's pronouncement was a knife in Yuri's heart. Betrayal of a friend and comrade could cut both ways.

***

Three days later Yuri returned with a plan of action. Sokolov read through the elaborately detailed scheme. When he reached the end of the report, he glanced up at Yuri and removed his reading glasses. He poured each of them a glass of vodka.

"No one can accuse you of not being ambitious, Yuri. Cheers!"

Both men drank up.

"We need a codename," Yuri said. "How does Operation Roswell sound?"

Sokolov shook his head. "We need something that will appeal to Shubin's childish sensibilities. We will call it Operation Minnie Mouse."

"Why Minnie Mouse?" Yuri asked.

"Shubin has the face of a rodent. It is also American. Shubin loves things foreign."

"Minnie Mouse it is," Yuri said.

All operations required a seal of approval from Director Shubin. His agency would be responsible for funding the operation and setting the plan in motion.

"This will be on its way by courier to Moscow first thing in the morning."

CHAPTER 11
In kind

Moscow

First Chief Directorate of Foreign Espionage Arkady Shubin puffed on a cheap Turkish cigar. It was a filthy tasting thing, hardly worth the waste of a match. In the current climate of a post-war Soviet Union, premium booze and premium cigars were luxuries no longer available. The Americans were the only ones who had benefitted financially from the war. Everyone else was broke. Still, you could get good cigars and good liquor, especially in Paris, if you were willing to pay. The only way to get such luxuries in the Soviet Union these days was by leaving the state on official business, an opportunity he was no longer afforded. Was it any surprise that travel budgets for his subordinate intelligence officers were through the roof?

In his day Shubin had once cut a dashing figure. He was well-educated, refined, and sophisticated. Prior to the war he had been given free rein to travel. He was the prize of the KGB. He had orchestrated assassinations, embedded moles, and successfully oversaw the theft of so many foreign secrets they were impossible to enumerate. As often happens with success, it came with a terrible price. Two years after the war, Arkady Shubin was promoted with rank and provided with an impressively appointed office in the Kremlin. His days of travel came to an end. These days he was a virtual prisoner of success and Soviet bureaucracy. How he missed those carefree days of rollicking in the great cities of Europe.

He stared at a mound of files on his desk. Every day an ambitious staff of junior officers sorted a stack of reports and recommended intelligence operations from both agents abroad and officers within the Soviet Union. Reports deemed worthy were then forwarded to Director Shubin.

Shubin casually sorted through the file folders. As was his habit, he pulled those files with unique sounding names. Otherwise there was simply too much paperwork to read through and far too many ridiculous schemes. Too many of these young post-war officers planned operations that seemed better suited for motion pictures rather than the actual business of espionage. Shubin pulled a file folder from the pile with the name Operation Minnie Mouse written across it. An interesting name, he thought. It was not necessarily original, but it was amusing. He opened the file folder. The report had come from Major Sokolov at Kapustin Yar. Sokolov was a well-respected soldier. Operation Minnie Mouse concerned the incident that had happened at Roswell, New Mexico, four years earlier. Sokolov's interest in the Roswell event was well-known among senior intelligence officers. It was an interest Shubin himself did not share. As far as he was concerned, Roswell was a case of collective lunacy. Shubin thumbed through the file. It contained clippings from American newspaper accounts, a brief analysis of the incident, and copies of the communiqués from a variety of agents. Sokolov had also supplied an extensive narrative that drew together all the separate strands of information. As always, Sokolov was thorough. Acknowledging both the hysterical aspect of the story and the possibility of hoax, Sokolov clearly and logically laid out arguments for and against an operation. In his final analysis, Sokolov recommended a full-scale operation be undertaken to infiltrate and extract. The appearance of the girl near Wright-Patterson Air Force base was too much of a coincidence. She had disappeared from Roswell and now she was near the secret facility known as Hangar 18. The Roswell event was simply shrouded in too much secrecy for the Soviets to ignore.

One item drew Shubin's attention. Sherlock Holmes and Dr. Watson had been on site the night of July 7, 1947. Sokolov noted that the presence of the English detective and his companion may have been entirely insignificant, or it might be further evidence of a much more involved matter and cover up.

Shubin closed the case file and turned his attention toward a framed photograph on his desk. The photo was of a smiling young woman on a sunny afternoon. Behind her, in the distance, stood the Eiffel Tower. From inside his desk drawer Shubin withdrew a rubber stamp. He flicked away the filthy tasting cigar and smashed the rubber stamp against the cover page of the file. In bold, red ink, the fresh imprint read APPROVED!

Shubin stared at the red APPROVED imprint for several minutes. He then set about amending details of the plan.

CHAPTER 12
The Tuesday Man

Kapustin Yar

Yuri Olenev was impatient for the overnight satchel to arrive. The courier from Moscow was overdue. Yuri plied himself with cigarettes and coffee. He had to admit to himself he was a nervous wreck. Yuri was young, but he was also ambitious. He felt most fortunate to have been assigned to Kapustin Yar. In his two years at the top-secret aviation site, he had quickly moved through the cutthroat business of promotion and achieving rank. His current assignment as personal aide to Major Sokolov was the cherry on top of the icing. He was fiercely loyal to Sokolov, one of the few Soviet officers Yuri regarded as a man of integrity. Even in a well-earned position such as his, one could never get too comfortable. There were always those who would slit your throat in an instant for an advantage. Trust lasted no longer than it took for one to better one's position. Yuri knew he was surrounded with equally ambitious junior officers. Envy was an elixir that fed treachery. Yuri's relationship with Sokolov was a source of jealousy in the ranks. He was careful never to overstep the bounds of propriety in his publically viewed dealings with the Major. But there were those who saw beyond Yuri's strict observance of protocol. If one took the time to observe, one could see Sokolov treated his personal aide with uncommon equity. Thus, it was always important to remind those of higher rank of one's worth. Hopefully the tardy courier would bring with him such a reminder.

Two hours after he was expected, the courier from Moscow finally arrived.

"Don't ask," he said, dropping his pouch onto Yuri's desk. "Weather and mechanical difficulties. One day, Yuri, we will do everything electronically. How? I have no idea, but I predict it."

Yuri laughed. Oleg Yermilov was The Tuesday Man. Each day of the week a different courier flew in from Moscow with a sack of mail, official correspondence, and communications designated as *eyes only*. Of the seven couriers, Oleg was Yuri's favorite. He was always good for a laugh. Over coffee Oleg would share the latest gossip from Moscow, smoke a cigarette, and then be on his way back to Moscow with a satchel full of documents for the Kremlin.

Yuri opened the pouch Oleg had arrived with. Inside was the cover page of Operation Minnie Mouse. As this operation had been Yuri's idea, it was most important the plan receive the blessing of Director Shubin. Yuri breathed a sigh of relief at the sight of the bold red imprint. His first operation had been given a go.

At the bottom of the page Director Shubin had added a brief handwritten note.

A commendable plan. We will contact Cherepanov to advise him when to expect a visit from babushka.

"Babushka." Yuri chuckled and shook his head. "These old guys."

Yuri went to The Hangar to share the news with the Major.

CHAPTER 13
Lights, camera, action!

London, 1952

"Cut!"

At once all action on set came to an abrupt halt. The authoritative voice had echoed across the giant sound stage of Shepperton Studios. The lights flooding the vast interior set extinguished. The whir of motion picture cameras wound down. Sound recorders were set to pause. A moment later Lawrence Meddings strode angrily onto the spacious interior set meant to represent a stately English manor in the latest Sherlock Holmes film adventure, *Moon Over Baker Street.* Attired in a high neck jumper, jodhpurs, and riding boots, Meddings cut a preposterously ridiculous figure. In place of a riding crop, the fuming director carried a megaphone. "Who in hell yelled cut?"

Silence descended over the scene. "I did," the previous voice said.

"Who is that?" Meddings asked of his assistant. "Who said that?"

Meddings' timorous assistant pointed to the group of onlookers.

The man standing to my side stepped forward.

"Sherlock Holmes."

"Mr. Holmes," Meddings said, putting down the megaphone and placing his hands on his hips. "I am the director of this film, the only director. I say lights, I say camera, I say action, and I say cut. I am the only person who says those things. I am the voice of God. You and Dr. Watson are here as technical advisers only. When I wish your advice, I shall ask for it. Could I be any clearer?"

"Quite right," Holmes said, belying no hint of apology in his voice.

"Thank you." Meddings turned to his crew of actors, cameramen, and lighting technicians. "Take twenty-seven. Mark. Lights." The scene lit up immediately. "Camera." Camera motors spooled up to speed. "Action." A tall fellow in a deerstalker entered the set, followed by a chubby fellow.

The actor playing Sherlock Holmes walked center and hit his mark. "This must be the place, Watson."

"Oh?" Said the actor playing my role.

"Yes, Monmouth Manor."

"Cut!" The commanding voice said again over the lines of the actors.

Immediately all action stopped once again, and lights dimmed.

"Bloody hell!" Lawrence Meddings rushed furiously onto the set. "Good God, man. Did you understand anything I said earlier?"

"As a matter of fact, I did. You were quite clear."

"Then why do you continue to disrupt this production?"

"Because you have it all wrong."

"Have it all wrong? Have what wrong?"

"Me. Watson. Do you think we would enter Muskrat Manor without knowing it was Muskrat Manor?

"Monmouth!" Meddings corrected. "It is Monmouth Manor."

"Whatever the name, an exterior establishing shot would have already conveyed that fact. Previous dialogue would already have established where Holmes and Watson were going. Why waste precious screen time repeating what everyone already knows? Sherlock Holmes does not walk into a manor and say, "This is the place." Of course, it is. Sherlock Holmes investigates. He discovers. He is not Lestrade. He does not waste time stating the obvious."

"Are you quite finished?" Meddings fumed.

"No. The chap playing Holmes is all wrong."

Meddings looked from Holmes to me.

"I must agree." I said, adding fuel to the fire. "The chap playing me is all wrong as well. He seems doughy."

"Doughy?" The actor portraying me said. "Are you saying I am fat?"

Before I could answer, Holmes chimed in. "That is exactly what Dr. Watson means, only he is too much the gentlemen to say it."

"Well, I never," the fictional Dr. Watson said.

"If you mean you have never missed a meal, I quite agree," Holmes said.

"Out!" Meddings screamed. "You are fired. Both of you." Meddings sought his timorous assistant. "Jacob, have these gentlemen shown out and escorted off the property."

Holmes glared at the nervous assistant. "Don't bother, we shall find our own way out."

And with that Holmes and I ended our short-lived careers as technical advisers for the next Sherlock Holmes and Dr. Watson adventure.

"I much preferred Basil Rathbone," Holmes said once we were off studio property and in search of a taxi.

"He has retired from playing Holmes," I reminded my colleague. "He and Nigel Bruce are on to other projects now."

"I can't say I blame them. The series was getting a bit long in the tooth."

"Do I look portly to you?" I asked.

Holmes ignored my question. He was preoccupied with locating a taxi.

Behind the heavily guarded gates we had just passed through were soundstages filled with forests, city scenes, and all manner of fictional settings. Outside, I could not help but note the ordinariness of our surroundings. No longer were we in Monmouth Manor, now we were just two chaps waiting for a taxi. Near the studio entrance stood two men each reading a copy of *The Times*, a milk dolly puttered by, a lorry stopped to unload its cargo at a nearby pub, and pedestrians came and went. It was a perfectly normal London day.

"Here comes a taxi now," Holmes said, waving his hand.

Before we could enter the waiting vehicle, a woman called to us from the main gate of the studio. She had been on set busily taking notes. "Mr. Holmes, I am so glad I caught you in time. Could you spare a moment?"

"We have a pressing engagement," Holmes prevaricated.

Other than my delivering a manuscript to my editor, Holmes and I had nothing on the docket. For weeks Holmes had been champing at the bit for a new case. As nothing had come our way, he reluctantly agreed to our serving as technical advisors for the latest Sherlock Holmes film adventure.

"Is this a matter of urgency?" I asked.

"Not urgency, Dr. Watson. But it is a matter of importance. If you could spare a moment of your time."

"Very well," Holmes acquiesced.

I waved the taxi on.

"There is a teashop around the corner," the woman said.

A few minutes later we were taking tea and coffee at a little teashop called *Scenes*. As the name of the establishment implied, the main clientele were employees of the film industry.

"Now, how can we be of service, Miss …?" I asked.

"Ransom. Abigail Ransom. I am continuity coordinator for *Moon Over Baker Street.*"

"Should this have something to do with the film, Dr. Watson and I are no longer in the motion picture business. It was all rather short lived, I am afraid. Most unsatisfactory."

"I saw what happened on set. I can't say I blame you. Larry Meddings is an insufferable bore. No Mr. Holmes, my request to meet with you has nothing to do with the film. It is an unrelated matter concerning an incident that happened five years ago. You have heard of the UFO incident in Roswell, New Mexico, during the summer of 1947?"

Holmes sighed wearily. "No pun intended, Miss Ransom, but this is not our cup of tea."

"Mr. Holmes, hear me out. Please."

Over the years Holmes and I had encountered no shortage of alarmists, conspiracy theorists, and individuals who had claimed to have seen flying saucers or had been abducted by aliens from space. All were immediately shown the door. Holmes had no patience for such tripe.

"We are familiar with the incident," Holmes said as a courtesy.

A great deal of time had passed since that night Holmes and I were diverted to the crash site. Other than a spate of wild rumors and conspiracies, nothing conclusive had ever been determined. Officially the crashed object was a weather balloon. The metal fragment Holmes had retained created some doubt in his mind, but most of what we currently knew we had learned from the newspapers. As Holmes would be first to say, doubt is not proof.

"Mr. Holmes, I am not prepared to say what did or did not happen that night. I was out of the country at the time working on a film. The incident made all the papers. Wildly varying accounts have emerged and frankly much of it sounds ridiculous, more akin to a Hollywood science-fiction film."

As if to indicate he wished our guest to get to her point, Holmes forestalled any further narrative on her part. "Miss Ransom, you do not seem the type to engage in conspiracy stories, thus I gather your concern relates to some other matter."

"Yes, that is correct Mr. Holmes. A young man and young woman went missing that night."

"Information that wasn't disclosed to the press until a few days later," Holmes said.

"If I recall," I added, "It was only after the crash site had been sanitized did the story of the young couple emerge."

"Also correct, Doctor."

"Miss Ransom, may we assume you have some connection to one of the missing young people?"

"The girl, Jenny Winston. She is my niece, and she is alive."

"Pardon me, Miss Ransom," I said with as much delicacy as I could. "The reports Mr. Holmes and I read in the papers first speculated the young couple had eloped. When nothing came of that angle, it was believed they had perished at the crash site. The incinerated automobile belonging to the young man was offered up as proof."

"Doctor, I work in an industry that creates illusions. In fact, I have had the good fortune to work with Alfred Hitchcock on three occasions. If I have learned anything, it is that our trust in the institutions we are taught to rely on is often misplaced. The car could have easily been torched by government authorities, after the fact, especially as no remains of any kind were found."

"Could not that have been due to the intensity of the fire?" I asked.

"Yes, that is possible; however, that theory emerged only after Abraham Carl, the local miner who first reported the story, said he may have seen Jenny and Lee that night."

"If memory serves," Holmes interjected, "not long after Mr. Carl gave his official story to authorities, he amended his eyewitness account to include seeing two humanoid creatures the night in question."

"Space aliens, wasn't it?" I said.

"Yes," Miss Ransom nodded. "And in that instant Abe Carl's credibility was gone."

"You must admit his story could not be taken seriously."

"I believe I see where Miss Ransom is going with this. It was only after the absurd claim by Mr. Carl that an alternate theory regarding the disappearance of your niece and her boyfriend was offered up. Mr. Carl was confused. He hadn't seen creatures at all that night. It was the couple he had seen."

"That puts a new light on matters," I said. "That could mean the young couple was alive after the crash."

"Yes, Doctor, but officials are now saying Abe Carl was confused due to the medications he was taking, in addition to his being an alcoholic. Government officials claim Mr. Carl had seen Jenny and Lee before the crash, not after."

"Intriguing to be sure," Holmes said. "But there is no way to establish the facts of any of this. The incident is five years old and the crash site has long been sanitized."

"I agree, Mr. Holmes. Whether by intent or circumstance, it is unlikely the authorities will reveal the truth. I have sought you out because of this."

Miss Ransom pulled a newspaper clipping from her coat pocket and unfolded it. It was a photograph of an attractive young woman in a crowd.

"This is my niece Mr. Holmes. This is Jenny. This photograph was taken over a year ago at a Fourth of July parade in Dayton, Ohio."

Holmes and I took a long look at the photograph of the young woman, surrounded by onlookers. The young woman held both hands above her eyes to shield her vision from the glare of the sun. I returned the clipping to Miss Ransom.

"It has been over five years. How can you be sure?"

"Dr. Watson, do you know what a continuity artist does?"

"Vaguely, I suppose."

"My job is to focus on detail and minutia. How much liquor was left in the glass two days ago? Where was it put down? How far down has a cigarette been smoked? How much ash remains? On which finger was the ring? On which wrist was the watch? I am very good at my job. I would not waste your time or mine on something I was not sure of."

"As Dr. Watson correctly points out, it has been five years. A young woman may change a great deal during that time."

"I admit the girl in the photograph is leaner in appearance and her hair is darker than the last time I saw Jenny."

"How can you be so certain?" I asked.

"If her appearance were the only factor, I would have to say in all honesty I could not be one hundred percent sure."

"The ring," Holmes said. "You recognize the ring on her left hand. It has a unique design."

"Yes," Miss Ransom said. "That ring was passed on by my sister to Jenny on her sixteenth birthday. It had been our mother's ring."

"You have no doubts about the ring?"

"None, Doctor. As Mr. Holmes pointed out, the design is unique. I would recognize it anywhere."

"You mention a sister," Holmes said.

"Yes."

"I am not clear why this matter has fallen to you. What efforts has your sister undertaken to find her daughter?"

"As I said, the incident in Roswell occurred while I was out of the country. I was in a remote location of South America on a film shoot when I learned Jenny had gone missing. A crewmember arrived with a bundle of newspapers some weeks old. As you might imagine, being sequestered in a remote jungle location, we were all hungry for news. That is how I learned the news of Jenny. By then she had been missing almost two weeks. The only way to contact my sister was by way of cable. I tried several times without success. Finally, a cable found its way to me from the sheriff's office in Roswell. It stated that my sister had passed away from injuries sustained in an automobile accident. My world simply collapsed."

"Is there a husband?" I asked.

"No, Doctor, he died during the war. It was just Jenny and my sister Margaret."

"Go on," I said gently.

"The film's director spared no effort in getting me out as soon as possible. I shall forever be indebted to him for his kindness. By the time I returned to the States, my sister had been buried. The sheriff shared with me all he knew about the accident, and then I read all I could about

74

the Roswell incident and Jenny's disappearance. I made innumerable inquires, all to no avail. Admittedly Jenny's disappearance had left some doubt as to what really happened to her, but I had no choice but to accept what had been reported and to get on with my life."

"And then you saw the photograph of the young woman you presume to be your niece," Holmes offered.

"Yes."

"How did you come across this photograph? Had it appeared in your local newspaper?"

"No, Doctor, it was sent to me anonymously. It appeared in a copy of the Wright-Patterson Air Force Base daily newspaper almost a year ago. As you can see she is a spectator in a crowd. The caption notes the occasion was a Fourth of July celebration."

"And you have only recently received this photograph?"

"Within the last week."

"You have no idea who would have sent this photograph to you or why?" Holmes asked.

Miss Ransom shook her head adamantly. "None!"

"Why wouldn't your niece have attempted to contact you? You are close, are you not?" I asked.

"Yes, Doctor, we were very close. That is what I cannot understand."

"Could it be your niece is under some form of protection?" Holmes asked.

"But why?" Miss Ransom replied. "Why would Jenny require protection? Why wouldn't she attempt to get in touch with me? I am at a loss to understand. It is heartbreaking."

"There, there," I said, patting Miss Ransom's hand.

Holmes steepled his fingers together and pressed them against his lips. "If your niece is in some sort of protection scheme, it may well mean she has been provided with a new identity."

"But why?" Miss Ransom asked with obvious exasperation.

"Information."

"What kind of information, Holmes?"

"Impossible to say, Watson. Whatever the young woman knows, we may assume it concerns the Roswell incident which has necessitated providing her with a new identity or protective custody."

"Do you believe your niece is being held against her will, Miss Ransom?"

"I have no idea, Doctor. I just wish to find her. It has been five years of agony and uncertainty." Miss Ransom turned to Holmes. "Can you help me locate my niece, Mr. Holmes?"

"I am entirely empathetic, Miss Ransom, but this is a matter for the Americans. The Americans do not look kindly on foreigners interfering in their internal affairs."

"The State Department has slammed every door in my face."

"I am sorry, Miss Ransom, we simply have no authority."

"Would it make a difference if I told you Jenny is a dual national?"

"Jenny was born in England?" I asked.

"Yes. Jenny's father was an American stockbroker working in London when he and my sister met. Jenny was born a few months before the stock market crash. After the crash, my sister's husband moved his family to the U.S. So, you see Mr. Holmes, Jenny is a British subject."

"I wish I could help, Miss Ransom, but this really isn't for us. I think you must work through an official agency. If I were you, I would begin with the British consulate."

My heart went out to Miss Ransom, but Holmes was resolute. He had no interest in taking on Miss Ransom's case.

"Mr. Holmes, I hope you will reconsider. I cannot stress to you how important this is to me." Miss Ransom placed a generously stocked portfolio on the table. "I brought this along in the hopes you would agree to help me. It contains every newspaper article and document I have been able to find related to the case. I have no further use for it. Thank you for your time, gentlemen."

After Miss Ransom exited the shop, I turned to Holmes. "I must say, Holmes, I am more than a little surprised. I felt sure you would take this on. As it is, we have nothing else on the boil."

"If the young woman in the photograph is Jenny Winston, there may be nothing nefarious about this at all. Perhaps the young woman sought a new life for herself."

"Of course, but doesn't the whole thing strike you as a bit odd?"

"Watson, you imagine the Americans are involved in some sort of cover-up or conspiracy. Why?"

"Clearly there is much more to this Roswell business than we are aware. We were there that night. It has always seemed to me a bit fishy."

"You know as well as I, there is always a perfectly logical explanation. Since we are not privy to whatever it is the Americans do not wish us to know, I have no intention of wasting time with idle speculation."

"Is it possible, as ridiculous as it may sound, the Americans actually discovered an alien spacecraft? And that is why it is so important to keep that information under lock and key."

"Watson, we have only the word of a discredited alcoholic. You and I saw nothing that evening that would suggest such a scenario. Whatever unanswered questions there may be, it is not up to us to answer them."

As we exited the teashop, Holmes stopped abruptly. "The portfolio, Watson. It is still on the table."

I retrieved Miss Ransom's portfolio and waited with Holmes for a taxi. As our taxi pulled into traffic, I noticed the two men I had seen earlier outside of the studio now standing together at the bus stop adjacent the teashop. They still had their heads buried in copies of *The Times*. "It's a wonder those chaps don't bump into each other, what with their heads buried in their papers like that."

"Yes," Holmes replied. "The same thought occurred to me as we passed by."

CHAPTER 14
Anniversary

Moscow

Another anniversary had passed and still there was no promotion, no pay raise, nor official commendations. Tatiana Andreyev had been both loyal and a hard worker. After almost three years in her position as a photo analyst, none of what she had been promised materialized. She had distinguished herself far more than the other girls who shared her cubicle, yet the pats on the back from her immediate supervisor and promises of commendations had still produced nothing. Her position and status were exactly as they had been the first day she joined Soviet intelligence. The other girls seemed not to have noticed such oversights. Their lives were filled with the distractions of boyfriends, romance, and marriage. Not that those things were not important to Tatiana, but she saw them as complementary to her desire to succeed in her own right. For more than a year, Tatiana had been keeping a list of every report she had submitted to her supervisor, noting the date, time, and particulars. Every report elicited the same response: "Well done, Comrade. Your good work will be noted and rewarded."

Tatiana summoned her courage and went to her supervisor. She presented the handwritten note her supervisor had attached to the receipt of her latest report.

"When, Comrade Supervisor?"

"What?" The elder woman scowled.

Tatiana placed the handwritten note on her supervisor's desk. "I mean no disrespect, Comrade Supervisor, but you have encouraged me with your supportive words for almost three years and nothing has changed."

The woman pulled off her glasses secured by a chain and let them fall about her neck. "Are you accusing me of impropriety?" The woman's cold grey eyes narrowed.

"I am not. Yet nothing has come of my many reports. I have kept a record of day and time."

"You keep records?"

Tatiana nodded.

"Comrade, you will excuse me for a moment."

Tatiana watched her supervisor go to her desk and pick up the telephone. After a brief conversation, she returned to the photo analyst, whose knees were knocking.

"We have an appointment with First Chief Directorate Shubin. Collect your documents and meet me outside of his office in fifteen minutes."

Tatiana felt positively sick to her stomach. Shakily she made her way to the ladies' room and patted her face with cold water. What had she done? What had she been thinking? Could she run away? No, she had made her bed. She had no choice but to follow through. Perhaps Director Shubin would understand, after all he had a reputation for fairness.

Fifteen minutes later Tatiana Andreyev found herself standing in front of Director Shubin's desk.

Tatiana's supervisor wasted no time getting to the point.

"Comrade Director, this young woman is Tatiana Andreyev. She is assigned to photo analysis. She believes I have treated her unfairly, that my commendations of her work have been insincere."

Tatiana felt as if she would faint.

Shubin sighed. He had little patience for these intra-agency personnel squabbles. He would have dismissed the old crone immediately were it not for the fact that she was the wife of a senior official. Even though he himself was more senior, it wasn't wise to make enemies, as this attractive young woman had already done for herself.

"What have you to say for yourself, Comrade?"

Without placing blame, Tatiana made her case to Director Shubin. It was a matter of fairness.

"Comrade Supervisor, let us step outside for a moment."

Shubin already knew what his answer would have to be. He needed some fresh air and to send this most disagreeable old woman on her way. She offended him as much as the filthy Turkish cigars he was forced to smoke.

When the office door closed behind her, Tatiana's legs buckled. She grabbed the edge of the director's desk for support, accidentally knocking over a small photo frame. Nervously she picked up the photograph. She stared at the image of the smiling young woman. Years of training immediately set the wheels of her vast photographic memory in motion. It was a face she had seen before. She returned the photograph to its place on the director's desk and froze the image of the young woman in her mind, filing it away in a temporary folder.

Shubin reentered his office. Tatiana turned to face her superior.

"Comrade, an organization such as ours depends on unquestioned loyalty. That you have called into question the actions of your immediate supervisor raise concerns about the quality and depth of your loyalty to the state. Reward is in the work we do here; we do not work for reward. You are compensated appropriately, and you are commended for your good work. You are due no obligation beyond that. I will not recommend disciplinary action. You may be sure, however, that you have made an enemy of your supervisor, and that will be discipline enough. You are dismissed."

Tatiana thanked the director and returned to her floor. She wanted to cry, but that would have to wait until she got home. She would not give her supervisor the satisfaction of seeing her tears. As for Shubin, without question he could have treated her more harshly. His talk of loyalty and intrinsic reward meant nothing.

Loyalty was reciprocal. Reward fostered loyalty. You could not demand of others what you were not willing to give. Angry as she was with herself for being naive, Tatiana was angrier with Shubin and the state.

Over the next several days Tatiana replayed the image of the smiling girl in the photograph over and over in her mind. At last she found what she was looking for. It was a photo and article from *The Times* six years earlier. Ellen Sharpe, a female employee of the de Havilland Aircraft Company, had been arrested on charges of industrial espionage. Her arrest came after a lengthy investigation into the passing of highly classified aircraft designs to the Soviets. An unnamed and unidentified Soviet agent contacted Miss Sharpe during two known holiday visits to Paris shortly after the war. As of Miss Sharpe's sentencing, the identity of the Soviet agent remained a mystery.

Tatiana studied the photograph of the young woman for some time. She went so far as to make a copy of the photo and take it home with her. She felt a kinship with the young woman serving time in a British prison. In some way, wasn't she herself a prisoner in the windowless basement of the Lubyanka Building? She had no future. Hadn't they both had a right to expect more from Arkady Shubin?

She imagined those carefree days in Paris. How alive Ellen Sharpe must have felt. She thought about the thousands of photographs she had analyzed over the years. There were images of exotic locations, intriguing people, and wonderful fashions. Tatiana Andreyev arrived at a decision.

After clearing away her dinner dishes, Tatiana withdrew the copy of the photo from her handbag. She looked at the photograph of Ellen Sharpe and spoke to it as if Ellen were present. "Well, young lady, you may not know much about misplaced loyalty, but I do. Perhaps one day you will thank me." With a pen, Tatiana wrote *With Love, Arkady Shubin* across the photo. As an afterthought, she turned the photograph over and quickly scribbled something across the back. Then she sealed the photograph in an unaddressed envelope. On her way to work the following morning, Tatiana Andreyev dropped the envelope into the letter slot of the residence of the British Ambassador to the Soviet Union.

CHAPTER 15
A change of mind

London

More than a week had passed since Holmes and I met with Miss Ransom. I had not seen Holmes since I exited our taxi at my flat in Belgravia. My attention was fully devoted to manuscript revisions insisted upon by my new editor. My previous editor with whom I had shared a long acquaintance had recently announced his retirement. Promoted in his place was a handsome woman I guessed to be in her early forties who assured me she had the greatest respect for her former colleague, but wanted it known she had ideas of her own. As such, time had not permitted my dropping in on Holmes and the matter Miss Ransom had brought to us had drifted far from my thoughts. Upon delivering my revised manuscript to my new editor, Miss Eden Terry, I was shuttled into a private room with a typewriter, a portfolio filled with notes, and ordered to write an afterward to the manuscript I had just delivered as some of the essential details of the case had changed upon further inquiries by Scotland Yard.

The afternoon proved positively exhausting. Miss Terry was a relentless taskmaster, hovering over me as an impatient head mistress until I rolled out the final page and handed it to her. Believing I had been subjected to Miss Terry's worst, I rose to leave, desperately in need of a stiff drink. To the contrary, the worst was yet to come.

"Dr. Watson, I believe we must address your narrative style."

"Oh?" Goodness, how I wanted that drink.

"Your narrative style feels distant. It doesn't feel inclusive. It keeps one at arm's length."

"Miss Terry, your predecessor Mr. Wilburn never expressed such sentiments. My style is the same today as it has always been."

Miss Terry's eyes lit up. "Exactly, Doctor! You have struck upon what I am getting at. We live in a changing world. Styles change. Readers change."

"I am aware that time marches on and change is inevitable. Rather than beating about the bush, Miss Terry, what specifically are you driving at?"

"You do realize, do you not, more and more women are reading your stories."

"As I have been told."

"And we most certainly wish to build upon that audience."

"Meaning?"

"Perhaps a little more appeal to your female readers."

I couldn't think what Miss Terry meant. After several moments, I asked, "How does one go about that, Miss Terry? I have no idea how to appeal more to a female sensitivity."

"Perhaps you and the fictional Mr. Holmes can be a little more approachable."

"I am sorry," I said, massaging my forehead, "I am not following."

"Good lord, Dr. Watson, I am speaking of sensuality. Play to your readers. Play up that aspect. Women love that sort of thing."

The breath positively left my lungs.

"Without even trying, on the page you and Mr. Holmes are very — how shall we say — sexy characters?"

"Great Scot, woman, what are you asking of me? Are you asking me to write something salacious?"

"Of course not! I am merely recommending less formal and more approachable protagonists. Add more appeal to the intrigue and I am quite certain sales will increase."

I was completely flustered. "I don't know what to say."

"Come on, John. You don't mind if I call you John, do you?"

"No, Miss Terry, not at all."

"Now that we're on a first name basis, I prefer Eden to Miss Terry."

"Very well, Eden."

"In this post-war era, publishers are struggling to find their way. Readers are no longer embracing the writers and works they used to. I think Sherlock Holmes and Dr. Watson must change as well. I know I am asking a lot of you, but at least think about it."

Think about it? How could I? I felt utterly discombobulated and clammy.

"You will think about it?"

"Yes," I blustered.

"Good. Now, may I buy you a drink?"

I glanced at my watch.

"Holmes?" Miss Terry asked presciently.

"I should check in." I removed my overcoat from the coat rack and slipped into it.

"A raincheck then." Miss Terry handed my hat to me. "It's a brave new world, John."

"Indeed," I said hurrying from her office.

Once outside, I fell back against the wall and drew a deep breath. My pride had been wounded. I was not used to having my writing critiqued in such a bold fashion. Miss Terry was quite forward; her remarks had seemed personal. I held out my hand. It was shaking. Was it anger? After a few moments I had to admit to myself no,

86

I wasn't shaking from anger. I wasn't angry with Miss Terry at all. She was doing what every good editor ought to do. It was something altogether quite different and unexpected. I was rather taken with Miss Terry.

I collected myself, exited onto St. James Street and hailed a taxi.

Upon arriving at 221B, I let myself in, looked in on Mrs. Hudson and then entered Holmes apartment without knocking. I stopped short in the doorway. Holmes's study was filled with odd-looking scale model aircraft, blue prints, and renderings of unusually shaped flying objects.

Holmes glanced up from what seemed to be a scale model of an airplane wing. "Watson, old fellow, you look positively flushed. I'll have Mrs. Hudson bring in some tea."

"I have just spoken with her. She is preparing a pot now."

"Excellent! Have a seat. Judging from your appearance, I should guess all did not go well with your editor."

"How could you possibly know?"

"You have what I presume to be typewriter ink on your fingers. As you were due to deliver a manuscript this week, I must assume you have just come from your publisher."

"A most trying afternoon, Holmes."

"Judging from the scent of perfume hanging on you, it seems Mr. Wilburn has taken to wearing *Bellodgia*."

"What? No! Wilburn is out. He has retired."

"In his place we may assume a far more attractive editor, which no doubt accounts for the flush around your neck."

"I prefer not to discuss the matter. Now tell me about this sudden interest in aviation."

Holmes waved his arm as if to introduce the array of models and miniatures around him. "I have immersed myself in a study of aerodynamics. One simply cannot apprehend the concept of the flying saucer unless one understands the principles of aerodynamics and a propulsion system capable of powering such a craft."

"Holmes, are you expressing a belief in flying saucers?"

"No, Watson. I am attempting to understand the plethora of reported sightings worldwide."

"Mass hysteria? Delusion? Natural phenomena?"

"Hard to say. Accounts of the first sightings reach back as far as biblical times."

"How reliable could those reports be? The ancients were hardly equipped with the language to accurately describe celestial events. In those days of pre-science, were not such sightings typically explained in a religious context?"

"True. But even with a contextual language, many modern sightings defy explanation.

"I have yet to understand how Stonehenge was created. I think we must accept that there are things in this world that defy explanation. Why worry about that which is simply beyond our understanding?

"Sightings appear to occur in cycles. Do you not find it unusual that the most recent cycle of sightings comes on the heels of World War II?

"Since the war, aviation technology has evolved considerably. I have no doubt these modern sightings are experimental craft. It certainly occurs to me that what we witnessed in Roswell could be. Isn't every country capable of producing aircraft developing its own technologically advanced weapons and aviation?

"What do you make of the Americans taking the lead in compiling and classifying sightings under the auspices of Project Bluebook?"

Mrs. Hudson arrived with tea, allowing me a moment to consider Holmes's question.

"Those ancient sightings, how can we possibly know? A meteor or a comet could easily account for such occurrences. In these modern times, sightings are far more problematic. If we subscribe to the belief that modern sightings are man-made aircraft, why the need for a Project Bluebook?"

"Why indeed, Watson?"

I waited for Holmes to follow up his question with an answer, but he did not.

"Well," I said. "Intriguing to be sure, but I cannot imagine this sudden interest is not without a reason."

"I have decided to take on the Ransom case."

"A most unexpected turn of events. What has prompted your change of heart?"

"This case is intended for us."

"Intended? By whom?"

"That is to be determined."

"You believe there is more to this case than that of one missing young woman? Do you question the veracity of Miss Ransom?"

"My sense is there is more to this than Miss Ransom was at liberty to reveal."

"Go on."

"Any number of government agencies is better equipped to handle this matter than we, and yet she was insistent on my involvement."

"You have a reputation for solving perplexing cases. Something has set you off."

"You recall the day we were unceremoniously asked to leave Shepperton Studios?"

"Of course, the day we encountered Miss Ransom."

"Two men reading newspapers were standing near the studio entrance when we exited and hailed a taxi."

"After our visit with Miss Ransom, the same two men were at the bus stop outside the teashop. I remarked that it was a wonder they did not collide with each other as their faces were buried in the newspapers they were reading."

"Both men were reading identical issues of *The Times of London*."

"On any given day all Londoners are reading the same issue of *The Times*."

"Yes, but these gentlemen were reading identical issues that were at least two weeks old. I distinctly recall the headline."

"That does seem suspicious."

"It nags at me, Watson. Miss Ransom or we were being followed. The question is why? Loose threads inevitably lead back to the tapestry whence they came."

"You amuse me, Holmes, when you wax poetic."

"Miss Ransom's plea for our assistance is cast in a new light. Someone else has an interest in this matter."

"Let no challenge go unheeded, eh?"

"You yourself said we have nothing on the boil."

"If I may sound a note of caution, if there are agencies at work here, might we not be stepping into a trap?"

"I am convinced of it. We shall leave for America within the week."

"Holmes, you do realize that by taking on this case, we could well be taking on the government of the United States."

"Of course. One only hopes the Americans are up for it."

CHAPTER 16
Rescuing Jenny Winston

Ohio

Having concluded arrangements for my indeterminate absence with my housekeeper, Mrs. Portland, I met Holmes at London Airport for our journey to America. The long flight allowed plenty of time for the two of us to work through a scheme for locating Jenny Winston.

"Shouldn't finding this young woman be akin to searching for the proverbial needle in a haystack?" I asked. "Other than the newspaper photograph, we have nothing more to go on."

"Then we shall begin with the photograph. Note the photo credit, Watson. It reads courtesy of *The Dayton Herald*. That means the photograph was shared by another publication. It is entirely possible the photographer who took this picture may have additional photos in his possession. If so, those photos could well provide us with useful information."

"Of course," I said to myself. So often there was no magic in Holmes's methods. Simply, nothing escaped his notice.

Holmes and I overnighted in New York before flying on the next day to Dayton, Ohio. As Holmes was enough of a celebrity to enjoy name recognition, we both felt he should employ an alias for routine activities. For the immediate future, Sherlock Holmes would be Sherrod Hall. For my part, it was not necessary to assume an alias. My name was common enough. I would simply dispense with the title of Doctor. I would now go about my business as John Watson. After flirting with various cover ideas, we settled on insurance investigators for Lloyds of

London, thereby allowing us to make inquires and ask questions without arousing suspicion

After arriving in Dayton, we arranged for a modest hotel near Wright-Patterson Air Force Base. Early the next morning we traveled by cab to the offices of *The Dayton Herald*.

After establishing our credentials, we asked to meet with the photographer who had taken the photo of Jenny Winston. A few minutes later we were introduced to Paul Martin, a young man who seemed barely old enough to shave. Holmes came quickly to the point.

"If this young woman is who we believe her to be, she is entitled to a substantial insurance settlement. We are attempting to locate her. She may be using an alias. Do you have a name and address? I assume you require a permission whenever an individual's photograph appears in your newspaper."

"In the case of individual shots, we require a release. But in a crowd shot such as this it is not possible to obtain a release from everyone."

"What about the location? Is there anything you can tell us about the area where you took this photo?" I asked.

"Centennial Park. It has been an Independence Day parade route for years."

"Is it possible the young woman lives nearby?" I asked.

"Mr. Watson, I wish I could help you, but I would have no idea. This parade is a tradition that draws crowds from all areas of Dayton. I couldn't venture a guess."

"Of course," Holmes said. "Is this the only photograph you took that day?"

"Oh, no. I shot an entire roll of film. Truthfully, the photo chosen by my editor was the least interesting of all of the photographs I took."

"Why do you think your editor chose that photograph," I asked.

"You will have to ask him. He gave me the assignment. I wanted to take pictures of the parade. He said he wanted pictures of the crowd, lots of pictures. He was adamant. Beats me what he saw in it."

I wondered if Holmes was thinking the same thought as I. Instead of a random photograph, was the photo of Jenny Winston intentional? If so, why?

"If you were given the assignment of taking photos, why did this photograph appear in the Wright-Patterson daily newspaper?" Holmes asked.

"It's a common practice. Plenty of my photos have appeared in the base newspaper. News services make their photos available to other publications, especially if there is a specific interest. In this case, Wright-Patterson had a very impressive float in the parade."

"And yet no photos of the parade appeared in that publication," I pointed out.

"I shot plenty of them. You're quite welcome to have a look at my contact sheets."

"Yes, we would like that," Holmes said.

"Give me a minute."

Mr. Martin went into an adjoining room, pulled open a large file drawer, and returned with two contact sheets. He spread both sheets onto a conference table and provided us with a pair of yellow grease pencils.

"You may use the grease pencils to mark on the contact sheets. I'll leave you to it, then," the youthful photographer said. "I will be in the lab should you need me."

After thanking Mr. Martin for his help, Holmes and I sat and began poring over the contact sheets.

"What exactly are we looking for, Holmes?"

"Perhaps nothing."

"Right, let's get to it then."

With a yellow grease pencil, Holmes circled some individual shots and put an X through others. Methodically he winnowed down the number of photos he was interested in to five. Jenny Winston featured prominently in four of the five photographs. "Hmm," he said, sitting back in his chair, fingers steepled under his chin.

"Something?" I asked.

"Yes." Holmes pointed to a young woman in the original photograph. "Notice this young lady standing near Miss Winston. This same young woman appears in the four additional photographs. In photos two, three, and four, the crowd has thinned considerably, yet both this young woman and Jenny Winston remain close to each other. What does that suggest to you, Watson?"

"Could be coincidence, or it could mean the young women are acquaintances."

"Now consider this last photograph."

In the fifth photo, the crowd had all but dispersed. Jenny Winston was nowhere to be seen. But the other young woman was leaning casually with her back against an automobile, as if she were waiting for someone. The driver's side window was open. The young woman's elbow rested on the open window panel.

"Perhaps the young woman owns the car."

"My thoughts as well," Holmes said. He moved his finger to the automobile's license plate number. "Please ask Mr. Martin to rejoin us with a magnifying glass."

Holmes pointed to the photograph of the young woman leaning against the automobile. "Mr. Martin, why did you take this photograph? Do you know this young woman?"

"No," the young man allowed. "My instructions were to take crowd photos. Crowd shots are boring."

"I see," I chuckled. "You were bird watching."

Mr. Martin blushed. "I am afraid you have me there, Mr. Watson."

Holmes held the magnifying glass over the photograph. "Jot down these numbers, Watson."

We thanked Mr. Martin for his help and made our way to the Dayton department of motor vehicles. After waiting an inordinately long time, we pled our case to a skeptical clerk who noted our request was highly irregular. As we were seeking restitution for damage to my vehicle while parked at the local A&P, and as a concerned witness had provided us with the license plate number of the offending vehicle, the clerk waived protocol this time and provided us with the name and address of one Jessie Brandon.

Later that afternoon we arrived at Miss Brandon's home. The young woman's mother answered the door. After explaining the purpose of our visit, Mrs. Brandon confirmed her daughter did indeed know the young woman in the photograph. However, she was not comfortable releasing the young woman's address. The young Miss Brandon saw no harm in providing the address of the friend she knew as Clare Simmons. Mrs. Brandon was adamant. She would not permit her daughter to accede to our request. At that point Holmes was forced to turn on the English charm. He resorted to a vulgar display of flattery in which the elder Brandon turned to putty. After agreeing to coffee, cake, and casual chitchat about England, we were finally in possession of the information we sought.

"Good lord, Holmes," I said on our return trip to the hotel, "you were positively shameful."

"Yes," Holmes remarked. "I did not enjoy that. The cake wasn't very good, either."

The following day over lunch, Holmes and I mapped a strategy for meeting Jenny Winston. According to Miss Brandon, Jenny Winston was employed and usually did not arrive home until sometime after six. Before embarking on our trip, we had previously selected several family photographs from Miss Ransom's portfolio. We knew to expect some incredulity on the part of Miss Winston. Our hope was to minimize the shock as much as possible. How Miss Winston would wish to proceed would be entirely up to her. If she wished to return to England to be reunited with her aunt, we were willing to serve as her escorts. Should she choose to remain in the U.S., we would honor that request and pass along whatever information she wished to share with Abigail Ransom. Of paramount importance was obtaining the assurance that she was not being held against her will.

By the time we arrived at Jenny Winston's house on Oak Street, daylight had turned to dusk. Unsure of how long our meeting would take, Holmes decided against having the cab driver wait.

Jenny Winston lived in a quaint little house on a picture-perfect street. A blue two-door 1941 Ford was parked outside. It was a Norman Rockwell painting of a quiet and sedate post-war America on the rebound.

Holmes pressed the doorbell. A figure appeared behind a pane of prism glass in the front door. The door opened to reveal Jenny Winston.

"You must not have read the sign," Miss Winston said discourteously. "No solicitations. Take your pamphlets and peddle them elsewhere."

"We are not soliciting," I replied. "I am Dr. John Watson, and this is Sherlock Holmes."

The young woman's eyes widened. "What?"

"May we come in, Miss Winston?" Holmes asked.

"No, you may not."

"We have some important information, Miss Winston," I said.

"I am afraid we must insist," Holmes said.

"Insist?" Miss Winston said indignantly. She reached into a small alcove to the right of the door and withdrew a baseball bat. "I don't know you from Adam, so you need to hit the road before I hit a home run on your heads."

"We've come at the request of Abigail Ransom," I said.

"Who?"

"Your aunt in England, Abigail Ransom," I added.

"Should you desire, we are here to convey you back to England," Holmes said.

Miss Winston's mouth fell open. "Good God! Tell me this is a practical joke."

Holmes produced his identification. "I assure you it is not. May we?"

Miss Winston leaned through the front door and looked both ways up and down the street. "Quickly!" She said, ushering us inside and slamming the door behind us. She pointed the way to her living room. "Don't bother taking off your coats, you won't be staying." She reached for a cigarette case above the mantle. "You shouldn't be here," she said, shakily lighting the cigarette she had withdrawn from the case. "Please leave!"

"What are we to tell your aunt?" I asked, baffled by the young woman's hostility.

"I can't explain. All I can tell you is you have made a mistake. You need to leave immediately. There is a back way out that leads on to an alley."

Before Holmes and I could press our case further, the front door blew open. Two men burst in and set upon all three of us. A moment later, the back door exploded open and a huge man rushed us from the opposite direction. The events of the moment proceeded so quickly I could not determine if guns were present. The two men who had entered through the front door grabbed Miss Winston while the big man who had come from behind hit me with such force he sent me reeling against the fireplace. Fireplace tools scattered across the floor as I collided with the mortar surround. Immediately the big man went for Holmes. The girl kicked and screamed as her assailants pulled her from the living room and through the front door. The man on Holmes was so much bigger that he easily overpowered my colleague. He threw a punch so hard that Holmes's legs turned to jelly. The brute began dragging my barely conscious friend to the front door. Outside a car horn blared anxiously. Shaking off the effects of my collision with the fireplace, I grabbed a poker from the set of tools that had spilled onto the floor. As the big man attempted to pull Holmes outside, I smashed the poker across the giant's face. He recoiled in agony, releasing his grip on Holmes. Holmes crashed to the floor with a thud. With blood streaming down the front of his face, the brute reached inside his coat for a pistol. One does not forget the lessons one learned in war. Before the hellhound could produce his weapon, I bore down on his arm with the full force of my fury. Bone cracked under the force of the poker and a shot rang out. Instantly a spray of crimson issued forth from the assailant's leg. The wounded man screamed and staggered through the front door toward the waiting car, its horn continuing to shriek its anxious alarm. With the girl and her odious malefactors aboard, the car sped away.

I helped Holmes to his feet, addressed his injuries, and poured two stiff whiskeys from the bottle the girl kept above her refrigerator.

"That was a rum go," I said after we had gathered our wits.

"Indeed," Holmes said. "Almost as taxing as our visit to the DMV."

Minutes later more visitors arrived. This time they were friendly.

CHAPTER 17
A bigger picture

Washington D.C.

Holmes and I were conveyed to Wright-Patterson, interrogated extensively, and then shuttled onto an unmarked military transport plane and flown to Washington D.C. the next day. Without a proper night's sleep, neither of us felt particularly chipper. Upon arriving in Washington, we transferred to a drab green government vehicle, threaded our way through morning traffic, crossed the Potomac and approached the capitol building. Our armed escort pointed through the window, "The United States Capitol, gentlemen. I guess you chaps — it is chaps, right? I guess you chaps aren't used to such regal and elegant sights like this."

Holmes and I turned slowly toward each other. I shook my head; Holmes could do no more than roll his eyes. Neither of us had the energy to suffer this fool.

Shortly we arrived at a long flight of steps behind the Capitol Building. "Here we are chaps."

Our escort exited the vehicle and stood on the passenger side with a hand placed carefully inside his coat under the left lapel. Holmes and I joined him. The man nodded for us to go up the steps. We ascended the steps and entered the large double doors. There another escort met us.

"This way, gentlemen."

The escort led us down a long hallway to an unmarked office. He knocked and then opened the door.

Holmes and I entered the large office. The door closed behind us. Inside were three men. One man was standing, another was seated at a desk, and the third was seated in the corner of the room with a notepad. The third man was present to ensure an accurate record of the meeting. He would not be introduced.

The man standing extended his hand. "Colonel Hawker, Mr. Holmes." He shook Holmes's hand enthusiastically. And then to me he said, "It is a pleasure, Dr. Watson."

"And the gentleman behind the desk?" Holmes asked pointedly.

Before Colonel Hawker could make the introduction, the man answered for himself.

"McCarthy," the man said rising. He walked from behind the desk and planted himself directly in front of Holmes. The two men were standing so close I thought their noses might touch. "Senator Joseph McCarthy." He stared directly into Holmes's eyes. I gathered the senator's stance was intended to assert his power, the object of which was to intimidate Holmes. I had to look away, fearing I might laugh.

"You may wish to go easy on the drink, Senator," Holmes said.

"What?" McCarthy said, stepping back as if he'd been struck. Reflexively he put his hand to his mouth and blew into it.

"No that is not alcohol on your breath, but something equally disagreeable."

"It is the pallor of your skin, the puffiness under your eyes. I would say you are in the advanced stages of liver disease."

"I don't care what you tea-sipping limeys think. Whoever you think you are, it cuts nothing with me. You've got a lot of explaining to do. As far as I'm concerned, you've committed an act of treason. In this country treason is a capital crime. And I'll be more than happy to pull the lever."

"In the strictest sense, treason is a betrayal of one's own country. Dr. Watson and I are British subjects."

McCarthy literally bristled. "We don't take kindly to foreigners."

Colonel Hawker raised his hand. "I'll finish up, Joe. You go on."

McCarthy had more to say, but the colonel occupied a position of influence well above that of a senator. McCarthy barreled through the office door, punctuating his indignity with a substantial slam.

"What a pugnacious fellow," I offered.

"His being here was a courtesy and nothing more." Colonel Hawker gestured for us to sit. "Joe is on a mission."

Holmes opted for a maroon winged back chair. "His reputation precedes him."

"Oh, that McCarthy," I said somewhat slow on the uptake. The long flight and lack of sleep were catching up with me.

Colonel Hawker pressed a button on his desk and spoke into what appeared to be a small radio. "Pauline, coffee for our guests. Please!"

"Does the senator believe we are communists?" I inquired.

"The senator thinks everyone is a communist. He sees them everywhere. I fear he may do a great deal of damage."

"Why allow him to continue?" I asked.

"He has a large constituency. In the current climate, opposing McCarthy is akin to supporting communism."

"Let us put your mind at rest," I said.

"No, Doctor, you and Mr. Holmes are not here because you are suspected of being communists."

"That's a relief," I said.

"No, I am afraid it is something far more serious."

"Excuse me?"

There was a knock at the door, followed by a young woman pushing a service cart with fresh coffee on it. "Will that be all?" The young woman asked.

"Yes, thank you Pauline." The young woman exited. "Help yourselves, gentlemen."

Holmes and I each poured a cup of strong, black coffee.

"My compliments, Colonel. Sumatra. Your dossier on me is quite accurate."

"We pride ourselves on having the best intelligence."

"Whitehall might disagree," Holmes said.

"What exactly are we being accused of Colonel?" I asked.

"First allow me to invite two other guests to join us." Colonel Hawker pulled open a section of bookcase that revealed a hidden door. A moment later two familiar figures entered Colonel Hawker's office: Mycroft Holmes and Abigail Ransom.

"I believe everyone has previously been introduced," Colonel Hawker said.

"Hello Sherlock," Mycroft said with his usual air of disdain for his brother

"Mycroft." Holmes met his brother's disdain with an equal amount of detachment.

"John, it's lovely to see you again as well," Mycroft said. "You remember Miss Ransom."

"Hello," Miss Ransom said, appearing slightly embarrassed.

Colonel Hawker gestured for Mycroft and Miss Ransom to sit.

"As to the matter at hand, I'll let Mycroft handle the British end."

"It seems, John, you and Sherlock have managed to assist the Soviets in kidnapping an American agent."

I turned to Miss Ransom. "Jenny Winston is an American agent? Did you not tell us the girl in the photograph is your niece?"

Miss Ransom glanced at Mycroft.

Holmes interceded. "We have been roped into a scheme, Watson."

"It is a wonder to me you didn't see the machinations behind all of this before now," Mycroft said.

Holmes chose to ignore his brother.

"He had misgivings from the start," I replied. "After our initial visit with Miss Ransom, Sherlock sensed something unusual about this case. All along he felt there was more to it than Miss Ransom was allowing."

"Watson, it isn't necessary to defend me."

Miss Ransom addressed herself to me. "I apologize for deceiving you and Mr. Holmes. I had no choice. Jenny Winston is my niece, but she is not the young woman in the photograph."

"She is one of ours," Colonel Hawker broke in.

Miss Ransom continued. "The young lady in the photograph bears a striking resemblance to Jenny. I haven't seen Jenny in five years. I could easily believe it is she. If I had any doubt, the ring was unmistakable. But I knew the girl wasn't Jenny."

"If you hadn't seen your niece in five years, how could you be sure?" I asked.

"Because I had spoken with both my sister and Jenny two days earlier."

"I am confused," I said. "You told us your sister died."

Ever impatient, Holmes was eager to move the narrative along. "Following the incident at Roswell, your sister and your niece were provided with new identities and relocated as a means of protection."

"Correct," said Colonel Hawker.

"Communication was strictly forbidden, Mr. Holmes. But one doesn't keep sisters apart. My sister first contacted me by letter and then by secure telephone. We speak from pay telephones at pre-arranged intervals. Both my sister and Jenny are safe and happy."

"What about the boy?" I asked.

"You will have to ask the Colonel."

"The boy was provided with a new identity. He and Jenny are no longer in touch. They have new friends and new lives quite apart."

Turning to Miss Ransom again, I asked how she had come into possession of the fraudulent photograph. Had it really been sent to her anonymously?

"No, that was a story made up for the benefit of you and Mr. Holmes. A man came to my flat. He was quite direct. He presented himself as a Soviet agent. He showed me the photograph and insisted the girl was Jenny. He said the Americans were holding my niece in protective custody. As I had spoken with my niece two days earlier, I knew this not to be true. I have no idea where my sister and my niece are located, but I knew neither was being held in protective custody. When I asked why this man was interested in my niece, he said Jenny was in possession of information vital to the security of the Soviet Union. He called himself Boris. Boris! I burst out laughing. I was convinced I must be the object of a prank. Boris assured me the matter was nothing to laugh about. He pressed me to confirm the girl in the photograph was Jenny. I told him I couldn't be positive. Then he showed me an enlarged portion of the photo that revealed the ring. There was no doubt it was Jenny's ring. How the girl in the photo had obtained the ring, I couldn't guess. I couldn't make heads nor tails of anything."

"Why didn't you refuse to cooperate with him and threaten to call the authorities?" I asked.

"He threatened blackmail. He said that since Jenny was alive and in an identity protection program, most likely my sister was receiving protection as well. Boris assured me it wouldn't take long to locate my sister. He was particularly threatening and dramatic. I had no way to determine if he could locate my sister and Jenny. Then he allowed that an operative known as The Caretaker was a particularly nasty piece of business none of us would wish to meet. The threat of blackmail didn't end there. He threatened my job in the film community."

"How so?" I asked.

"As a member of the Hollywood community, I associate with colleagues who have liberal ideas. Some are referred to as socialists. Others are called communists. I am none of those things; however, I have attended meetings as a matter of general interest and I have contributed to what I believe are worthy causes. The threat was simple: guilt by association. Given the climate of Hollywood these days, I am afraid studios err on the side of caution. One doesn't last long in Hollywood once the rumor mill is abuzz."

"Why contact Sherlock Holmes?" Colonel Hawker asked.

"I cannot answer that question. All I can tell you is my instructions were to make sure Mr. Holmes was involved. I was not to take no for an answer, otherwise there would be consequences."

"Why didn't you share this information when we met in London?" I asked.

"I was being followed. If what Boris said was true, I couldn't risk the discovery of my sister and niece and jeopardizing my career. I felt that if you knew the girl in the photograph was not Jenny, you would have no incentive to help me. When you sent me away from the teashop without an offer of help, honestly I wasn't sure what I would do."

"You may be assured your sister and Jenny remain quite safe," Colonel Hawker said reassuringly. "As for the Hollywood angle, a little tougher. But we will see what we can do. We will take things from here."

"Thank you," Miss Ransom said, rising from her chair.

"By the way Miss Ransom, how is the film coming along?" I asked. "*Moon Over Baker Street.*"

"It isn't. The studio pulled the plug. The official word is Holmes and Watson had no onscreen chemistry. The real reason is the script was discovered to have been written by a blacklisted writer using an alias. Goodbye, gentlemen."

Responding to a gesture from Colonel Hawker the note taker saw Miss Ransom out. A moment later he returned and resumed his task of taking copious notes.

"Pity that woman," I said. "It's a wonder she's held up under the pressure. I'd hate to think what would have happened had we not taken on this case."

"Miss Ransom comported herself remarkably well." Holmes turned to Colonel Hawker. "Now, Colonel perhaps you would like to provide Dr. Watson and me with the information we do not know. You surely cannot expect us to believe that an American intelligence agency that has gone to so much trouble to conceal the identity of a young woman and her mother would permit a photograph of that young woman to appear in a military newspaper?"

"Quite right, Mr. Holmes. The photograph was planted with the knowledge that it would most likely come to the attention of the Soviets. The young woman posing as Jenny Winston is Agent Piper Sands. She bears an uncanny resemblance to Miss Winston. Agent Sands was instructed to attend the Independence Day parade at Centennial Park. We arranged for a photographer from *The Dayton Herald* to be on hand to take pictures. We felt that a photo from a local newspaper would seem less suspicious than a photo that originated on base."

"So, Agent Sands was intended as a form of bait," I said. "For what purpose?"

"To expose a network of Soviet spies, Doctor."

"How long has this been going on?"

"Most people are of the opinion Soviet espionage is a recent phenomenon. The truth is the Soviets have been attempting to infiltrate all levels of American government and society since the late 1920s."

"The twenties?"

"Yes, Doctor, a common misperception. Working through a variety of intelligence services the Soviets have been engaged in systematic efforts to ferret out and pass along confidential information. Our friend McCarthy, overzealous as he may be, is correct in his assertions that Soviet agents exist in all strata of our government. They happen not to exist in the numbers he imagines."

"Have I been that naïve in my understanding of our relations with the Soviets?"

"Often the tensions between nations exist below the surface. Aside from the usual haggling over treaties and such, what really strikes at the heart of the matter are our fundamental differences in government. Those differences sow the seeds of a profound distrust, which doesn't mean we can't work together on occasion. But we are never going to see eye to eye. Our essential natures are too different."

"The Jenny Winston affair is not about undermining democracy," Holmes said.

"Our concern here is the defense industry, Mr. Holmes. It has always been a target for the Soviets. We have had varying degrees of success in protecting the existence of some of our most secret programs, as may be witnessed by almost identical weapons and aircraft. The Soviets have succeeded in stealing technologies for military vehicles and weapons, radar and guidance systems, as well as a complete set of design plans for our P-80 Shooting Star Fighter. They are masters of reverse engineering. Once something falls into their hands, the Soviets copy it quickly. We develop; they steal; we improve on the original."

"Seems like a tit for tat game," I observed.

"That's one way to put it, Doctor, but hardly a game. Since the end of the war the Soviets have stepped up their efforts to infiltrate those programs. Our use of atomic weapons to end the war with Japan set the Kremlin on edge. I am afraid both sides are developing weapons at an alarming rate, each trying to outdo the other with something bigger and more powerful."

"Let us not ignore the social aspect of their efforts," Mycroft added. "We see it in Britain all too clearly."

"To be sure, the Soviets are intent on subverting political and social life at all levels. Democracy is regarded as a threat, Mr. Holmes. Anything the Soviets can do to undermine our way of life is seen as a victory."

"Forgive me, Colonel, but I am losing the thread here," I said, trying my best to stifle a yawn. "This big picture you are describing, I am having difficulty relating it to Roswell."

Colonel Hawker continued his narrative. "We have been aware for a while now that we have moles in our midst. As you may well appreciate, we have a number of highly classified and highly sensitive programs."

"As do we," Mycroft interjected.

"Agreed. Agent Sands was our attempt to flush out as many of those moles as possible. This operation began well over a year ago. Agent Sands bears enough of a resemblance to Jenny Winston to fool most individuals. We know the Soviets meticulously comb our newspapers. They have an entire department of analysts devoted to news stories and photographs. We were certain the Soviets would eventually connect Agent Sands' recent photo with the five-year old photo of Jenny Winston."

"They could have easily missed it," I said

"Doctor, many operations fail in their objectives. We believed that once the Soviets made the connection, they would attempt to contact Agent Sands. The snag was we didn't know when it would happen, which is the reason Agent Sands was permitted to live off base. It was possible the Soviets would never make contact. Agent Sands is an independent and healthy young woman, and — well — it was impractical to confine her to the base. In the evenings she would leave the base in disguise. To create the impression Jenny Winston was being held in protective custody on the base, doubles were used to occupy the secured on base house where Jenny supposedly lived."

"You surely didn't think the Soviets would snatch her from base."

"No of course not. We had developed routines involving her leaving the base with an escort that would prove opportune times for a contact to take place. For example, a regular trip to the hair salon or the movies on a Saturday night."

"That seems a lot of trouble to go to for something that might never happen."

"Any less so than some of the fantastical operations conducted by the British during the war? Make no mistake, Doctor, we are at war, only this one moves at a slow and stealthy pace."

"You surely have agents here and abroad." I observed.

"We have not had much success inside the Soviet Union. We are grooming a young agent by the name of Cherepanov."

"A Russian?" I asked.

"American. About a year ago, we stumbled onto a sympathizer who had been passing along information to the Soviets. He quickly discovered we could be most persuasive. He broke under pressure and told us everything he knew."

"Did he reveal the mole?"

"No, he has no idea who the mole is. We are certain of that. We conveniently took care of the operative who had recruited Cherepanov. As no one in the Soviet Union has ever met or seen Cherepanov, we simply replaced their agent with our own. He is young, but not especially productive. We are receiving some intelligence from the Soviet Union, and he has passed along information we want the Soviets to see."

"The Soviets don't suspect anything?"

"Perhaps. It makes no difference. This is a game of percentages. You win some; you lose a lot. We all do. The life of an operative is short. The Soviets will remain in contact with Cherepanov until he is no longer worth their time."

"Did Cherepanov know of the plan to extract Agent Sands?" Holmes asked.

"He knew something was in the works, but not the date. He was told he would be advised when the operation would commence. He knows nothing of Agent Sands."

"What happened?" I asked.

"You and Mr. Holmes happened."

"How novel, using my brother to lead the Soviets to the girl," Mycroft said. "Rather than expending their own time and effort, the Soviets simply put Sherlock Holmes on the case."

"The Soviets believe Jenny Winston can tell them what happened at Roswell. Is that it?" I said.

"Yes." Colonel Hawker rose and walked to the window of his office. The Washington Monument gleamed in the distance.

"Colonel, you do know Holmes and I were at the crash site that night."

"Yes, Doctor, I am aware of that fact. You and Mr. Holmes were kept at a distance. I mean no disrespect when I say you and Mr. Holmes know nothing."

"We know that whatever crashed out there that night was not a weather balloon. Holmes has a small piece of the debris to confirm that."

"Merely a trinket, Doctor. That is all you have, and that is all you know."

I was tired of dancing around the issue of what Jenny Winston did or did not know. "What is the story of Roswell, Colonel?"

"I am sorry, Dr. Watson. Roswell remains classified. That information has never been released, nor will it be."

"What we saw that night clearly was not a weather balloon. It was some sort of a disc; that much was obvious. It was either one of yours, a Soviet craft, or it was an alien spaceship. As for the little green men, we didn't see any."

After a long silence, Mycroft spoke up. "As His Majesty's government has been drawn into this affair, I think we must consider how to effect the release of Agent Sands."

"Demand the Soviets release the girl immediately," I said.

"They will deny all knowledge of the affair."

"Holmes, how can they? The Soviets surely know the Americans know they are behind this."

"That is not how the game works, John." Mycroft said.

"The game, the bloody game. Lives are at stake and you boys play games." It was all I could do not to storm from the room.

"How much does Agent Sands know?" Holmes asked.

"About Roswell? Hardly anything, certainly nothing of use to the Soviets. But they will do their best."

"What about this fellow they call The Caretaker that Miss Ransom spoke of? What can you tell us about him?" Holmes asked.

"We have yet to identify him." The Colonel pushed a dossier across his desk to Holmes. "We know he is based in Moscow and travels extensively. Wherever he travels, he leaves behind a great deal of personal destruction. You will note his methods are most effective. We may reasonably assume Agent Sands has already been sequestered in a safe location. We may also assume The Caretaker has been notified. If he is currently in Moscow, he could be at any location in the United States within 72 hours. Should he be in Europe, Canada, or South America, his travel time will be less."

"Colonel, it seems to me this young woman is quite vulnerable." I couldn't imagine the young woman would fare well.

Holmes rose and began to pace the room. "The larger of the three henchmen who attacked us would have easily overpowered me and dragged me to his getaway car had Watson not intervened. The Soviets had more in mind than my merely leading them to Miss Winston. They wanted me as well. I think we must allow the Soviets to succeed. It may be the only way of returning Agent Sands safely."

"It is unclear what the Soviets had in mind for you, Mr. Holmes. However, since they now have what they came for they have no incentive to agree to a trade. You can be sure they know your knowledge of Roswell is limited."

"Then it was something else."

"But what?" I asked.

"My concern is what happens when the Soviets discover Agent Sands is of no value," Mycroft said. "Give Sherlock something of value to make the bargain worthwhile. Tell him what the Soviets want to know."

Colonel Hawker smiled with amusement. "Forgive me, Mycroft. You are really asking me to divulge to the British government classified information about Roswell."

"It was worth a try," Mycroft replied.

"Gentlemen, you must trust that our intelligence agencies will find Agent Sands. I am confident of that."

As he spoke, Colonel Hawker leaned over his desk, scribbled something on a small slip of paper and slipped it into his pocket.

"Colonel, your confidence in your agencies is admirable, but keep in mind you have a mole, perhaps several, within those agencies. Might they not prove the greater danger?"

"Mycroft, were the decision mine alone, I would enthusiastically authorize such an operation, but I have superiors to whom I am accountable. The prospect of allowing the British to run an operation within the United States will not fly. We have too many agencies and too many little men in charge of their respective kingdoms to placate. Even if it were possible, coordinating such an operation would be so cumbersome and time consuming we would lose the advantage of time. This really is our matter, gentlemen. We appreciate the offer of assistance from The Crown."

"Very well," Mycroft said. "Our business here is concluded. As always, Colonel, a pleasure."

As Holmes, Mycroft, and I rose to leave, Colonel Hawker had one more question. "I am curious, Mr. Holmes. Why did you agree to take on Miss Ransom's case? You obviously knew something was amiss from the start."

"Sport, Colonel. An Englishman cannot resist sport."

"A bit of the old game's afoot? Eh?"

"Something like that," Holmes said.

As Colonel Hawker walked us to the door, he slid a slip of paper into Holmes's pocket.

"Good luck, Mr. Holmes."

***

That afternoon in a very public Washington D.C. location, Holmes and I enjoyed a long, leisurely lunch together. We felt sure we were under continual surveillance. Holmes allowed our best chance of finding Agent Sands was for the two of us to split up. It was

116

impossible to know how many agents were tailing us. If we went our separate ways, perhaps we could divide the enemy long enough for Holmes to strike out on his own.

"Is that the best course?" I asked. "I worry for your safety, Holmes."

"I think we have no other choice," Holmes said. He reached into his coat and produced the piece of paper Colonel Hawker had slipped into his pocket.

"A telephone number?" I asked.

"I believe so, Watson. The letter C below the number is most likely Cherepanov, the agent of whom the Colonel spoke."

"Colonel Hawker was adamant in his view that finding the girl was an American concern. He was quite clear that he could not authorize our involvement."

"No doubt for the benefit of the note taker. The Colonel is correct in his observation that bureaucratic red tape will delay action. Add to that his concerns regarding security. Until this network of spies is exposed, Watson, I believe the Colonel is unsure whom he can trust."

"Good lord, it's a web of deceit and lies."

"Indeed, old friend. Those who would strike at the foundations of everything we hold dear, do so by sowing fear and distrust. We must be vigilant, Watson. Return to London as scheduled. I believe you will be safer there. In London, Mycroft can offer you protection."

"You believe I am at risk?"

"Until we know the full extent of what this case is about, I think we must be very careful. I will do my best to remain in contact."

Holmes casually scanned the restaurant for any patrons showing an undue interest in us.

"In a moment I will excuse myself to make a visit to the men's room. I will not bother to retrieve my coat and hat from the coat check. I will slip out the back door of this establishment. Good luck, Watson."

Holmes excused himself as I continued with my lunch. Fifteen minutes later I paid our bill and returned to my hotel.

CHAPTER 18
The Salt Flats

The incessant drone and vibration of engines jostled Piper Sands awake. Groggy and with an aching head, she found herself securely restrained in the middle seat of a Cessna Bobcat T-50. A pilot and copilot were visible through the gap in a makeshift curtain that separated the cockpit from the three seats behind them. Clearly, she had been sedated. Other than a raging headache, she felt no worse for wear.

"Hey!" Piper called out.

There was no response from the cockpit.

"Hey, Moe and Larry, I see you there. I need to use the ladies room."

The copilot pushed aside the curtain. "You'll have to wait."

"Easy for you to say, Larry."

"It won't be much longer. And my name isn't Larry."

"What happened to the big guy, Curly? Did Holmes and Watson get him?"

"Rest assured, Sherlock Holmes and Dr. Watson will be dealt with, as you will be dealt with."

The copilot turned away and pulled the curtain closed.

As cavalier as Piper Sands tried to present herself, she had to admit she was scared. The risks of this operation had been carefully laid out and every contingency planned for, all except one. Who could have foreseen the intervention of Sherlock Holmes? How had that happened? The attempted snatch was designed to take place in a public setting. Her personal residence was a closely guarded secret. Even the mole didn't know where she lived; otherwise she would have been snatched long ago. A great deal of effort had been undertaken to create the impression she lived on base. The use of a double and an elaborate security plan had been devised to allow her to live as normal a life as possible until Operation Deceive was completed. How the hell had Sherlock Holmes managed to find her? Give him credit for that, but not for the fact that he wasn't clever enough to know Soviet agents were tracking him. It wouldn't take long for the Soviets to discover she wasn't Jenny Winston. Piper dreaded to imagine what tools they had in their arsenal to make her talk. Whether she had anything useful to tell them or not, her future did not look bright. Piper's training had prepared her for almost every contingency. Being bound, drugged, and kidnapped was not one of them.

Twenty minutes later the plane began its descent. The landscape below appeared as a barren desert. Piper Sands hoped she was still in the United States. Could be Mexico. The sedative her abductors had administered had erased her grasp of time.

The Bobcat T-50 made a hard landing.

"Good God," Piper Sands yelled from the back of the plane. "Do you know how to fly this thing?"

Neither man responded.

The small plane whipped up a whirlwind of dust as it taxied to a stop.

The copilot threw back the makeshift curtain, pushed open the door, and waited on the ground, holding a pistol at the ready in case Agent Sands tried something silly. The pilot undid Piper's restraint and nudged her through the door. She stepped onto the wing and then onto the sandy runway. An old tin hangar nearby and a Mobil gas pump suggested she was still in the U.S.

"Over there," the pilot said. He pointed to the hangar.

"I hope there's a bathroom in there. A shower wouldn't be bad, either."

"You talk too much," the copilot said.

"You really know how to make a girl feel welcome, Larry."

"I told you, my name is not Larry."

"What is your name?"

"None of your business."

"Larry it is. And the little guy, he's Moe."

The two Soviet agents led Piper Sands into the dilapidated old building. It was filled with machinery, airplane parts, and room to park the Bobcat inside.

"This way," Moe said.

The agents led Piper through a door down a set of stairs that led to an area underground. She prepared herself to be locked in a dark and dank basement. Instead, she entered a spacious, well-appointed room. An identical room was next door.

"Your room is number one," said Larry. "You will find everything you need to make yourself comfortable."

"Not what I expected," Piper said. "If you think this will soften me up to make me talk, it won't. You won't get anything out of me."

"We don't want anything from you," Moe said sinisterly. "We are not the ones doing the interrogating. That will be left to The Caretaker."

"The Caretaker? Who is The Caretaker?" Piper asked warily.

Moe shrugged. "He has a reputation. He takes care of things. Enjoy your stay, while you can."

Piper Sands surveyed her surroundings. "I guess it could be worse."

"It will be, count on it," Larry said.

Having done their best to unsettle their captive, the two men returned to the upper area of the hangar, locking the basement door behind them.

"How long must we babysit this girl?" Larry asked.

"Two days, three days. Until the Caretaker arrives. He will be coming from Moscow. He won't be here any time soon."

"Is he really as bad as they say?"

"I have never met the man, but from what I hear, he is most effective. He will deal with the girl."

"Good! She has a big mouth," Larry grumbled. "She is most obnoxious. If she doesn't shut up, I may kill her before The Caretaker arrives."

"Forget her. Now, open the doors. I should park this plane inside."

CHAPTER 19
Holmes alone

After slipping out of the restaurant, Holmes disappeared into a crowd of pedestrians and made his way to the Carlton Hotel.

"Will you be staying long, Mr. Holmes?" The desk clerk asked.

"I am afraid my stay will be all too brief."

The clerk handed Holmes a room key. "Fifth floor. Room 517. Welcome to The Carlton. Enjoy your stay, Mr. Holmes."

"Thank you."

Holmes took the lift to the fifth floor, dropped the room key into a waste bin, and exited the hotel by way of the back stairs.

The following morning a Soviet agent posing as a housekeeper entered room 517. The bed had not been slept in; the towels were still fresh. Immediately she placed a telephone call.

Holmes had no time to create a disguise. Sans hat and overcoat, Holmes knew he was less likely to stand out. He went a step further by gifting his suit jacket to a panhandler who looked as if he needed a good coat more than he. Next, he popped into a local sporting goods store where he purchased a baseball jacket and baseball cap.

"Which is it?" The clerk asked. "Phillies or Cubs?"

"Excuse me?" Holmes asked.

"You got a Phillies cap and a Cubbies jacket. Neither of those teams has a snowball's chance in hell of winning the pennant. The smart money is on the Yankees to repeat. Me, I'm a Dodgers fan. I'm seeing Brooklyn go all the way."

"Where is Brooklyn going?"

"Are you kidding me? The World Series!"

"The series, of course!"

"I've got plenty of Yankees and Dodgers gear."

"I'll stay with the underdogs."

Holmes paid for his purchase and disappeared into the hustle and bustle of Washington D.C.

Our meeting with Colonel Hawker had left me uneasy. In such a climate, could Holmes be sure of Colonel Hawker's loyalties? The Colonel had expressed guarded confidence in Cherepanov. What about Cherepanov's loyalties? Was he entirely trustworthy? I felt as if we had entered a den of snakes devoid of protection. Which ones were harmless? Which ones were lethal? No longer were matters simply black or white. These shades of gray had introduced a confounding complexity to our relations with friend and foe. Perhaps the chaos and uncertainty that issued from these events was the point. Keeping one off balance ultimately undermined our trust in the values and institutions we had come to rely on for stability.

In his new role as ordinary Joe, Holmes needed a telephone. A bus or train station was out of the question. Those places would be crawling with agents. He decided on a place where it seemed least likely to encounter a Soviet agent: a coin operated Laundromat.

Holmes settled on the K. Street Washateria. With the assistance of an operator, he fed several coins into the pay telephone and connected to the number Colonel Hawker had given him. After three rings, the telephone at the other end picked up. No one answered.

"Hello?" Holmes said. "Hello? Hello?"

There was still no answer, but the call remained connected.

Holmes had no choice but to take a chance. "This is Sherlock Holmes. A Washington friend gave me your number."

The silence continued.

"I am calling from a Laundromat on K. Street. The name of the establishment is K. Street Washateria. I will provide you with the telephone number if you wish to call back. I will wait five minutes, not a second longer."

After another long pause, Holmes received a response. "The Wide Eye Café on Route 66. Tucumcari, New Mexico. Ten in the morning, the day after tomorrow." The line went dead.

Holmes had less than 48 hours to get to New Mexico. Two blocks down K. Street he found a bookstore. It was crowded, perfect for easily blending in with other patrons. He made his way to the travel section. There he found a travel guide with a driving distance chart. Washington D.C. to Tucumcari, New Mexico was approximately 1500 miles. Driving or taking a bus was out of the question. A train seemed hardly faster. He had to fly. The Washington area airports posed too much of a risk. Consulting the travel guide once again, he decided on Philadelphia. He would hire a car and drive to Philadelphia. Barring unforeseen delays, he should arrive in Philadelphia in less than five hours.

As Holmes was being pursued by the Soviets, rather than the Americans, he felt safe renting a vehicle and flying under his own name. His name was well known; his face was less familiar. Neither raised the least bit of concern from the clerk at the obscure rental agency from which he had hired a vehicle. The ticketing agent in Philadelphia recognized the name but said nothing. She was used to selling tickets to celebrities.

Shortly after midnight Holmes landed at English Field in Amarillo, Texas. The airport in Amarillo was the closest major airport to Tucumcari, which was 120 miles away. Holmes spent the night in a nearby motel called The Flight Line. The following morning, after consuming a quarter of what The Flight Line Café billed as a belly busting breakfast, Holmes made his way to a local airpark that offered various flying services. Holmes settled on Bob's Air Taxi. Bob advertised safe and courteous service to Tucumcari four times a day.

Bob had a long white bushy moustache permanently stained from years of chewing tobacco. He had been a World War I air ace too far beyond his prime to fly in World War II. By the time Holmes arrived in Tucumcari, he knew more about Bob than most members of Bob's own family. As Holmes was about to depart, Bob said, "Thanks for the business, Mr. Holmes."

Holmes drew up short. "I don't believe I introduced myself."

"You didn't have to. I recognized you even with the baseball jacket. If you don't mind my saying, there's only one reason a man of your reputation, dressed as you are, is flying with a feller like me."

"What would that be?" Holmes asked, curious about the crusty fellow he had been flying with.

"You're either on a case or someone is after you."

"You have a keen imagination, Bob."

"You know, I've seen all types throughout the years. I think I'm a pretty good judge of character." Bob handed Holmes a business card." If you need anything, Mr. Holmes, you call me, you hear?"

"Thank you, Bob."

Twenty minutes later Holmes found himself in the heart of Tucumcari confronted with a fair selection of motor hotels featuring colorful names. He settled on The Blue Bird. After registering, he took a much-needed shower. Later he walked along Main Street, otherwise known as Route 66. He easily found The Wide Eye Café, fixed its location in his mind, and returned to his motel room, where he fell into a deep, dreamless sleep.

At 10 a.m. the following morning Holmes sat alone in a booth at The Wide Eye Café drinking a cup of coffee. Periodically he glanced up at the clock above the counter.

"Hon, you're gonna stare a hole in that clock up there." A waitress in a white uniform and cap hovered over Holmes with a fresh pot of coffee. "More."

Holmes nodded.

"Are you going to eat anything, or not? You look as if you could use a meal. You need to get some meat on those bones."

"I will have a simple order of eggs and bacon, nothing man sized or belly busting, please."

"How do you like them?"

"Excuse me?"

"Your eggs. Do you like them like me, sunny side up? Or over easy?"

"Surprise me," Holmes replied with a wink.

"Sure thing."

When the waitress returned with the breakfast Holmes had ordered, she asked, "Phillies or Cubs?"

"Neither. If I were a gambling man, my money would be on the Yankees or the Dodgers."

"I'll bring you some more coffee," the waitress said with a smile.

The man reading a newspaper a few booths away had been watching Holmes from the moment he had entered the café. From his position he had a wide view of the street. After almost twenty-five minutes, he was satisfied Holmes was alone and not being tailed. The man slid into the seat opposite.

"The cap and baseball jacket are a nice touch," the man said.

Holmes ignored the comment. He was tired of talking about a sport he cared nothing about. "I wondered when you would make contact. If you hadn't done so in the next few minutes, I would have come to your booth."

"Was I that obvious?"

The young agent had a lot to learn.

"Victor," the agent said, offering his hand. "I go by Cherepanov, but that is not my real last name."

Holmes waved his hand. "Don't say anymore. The less I know of your identity, the better it is for you."

"Point taken. Have your breakfast, then we will go for a drive. I have a Jeep outside."

Holmes finished his breakfast of manageable portions, after which Victor Cherepanov drove Holmes to a desert location a few miles from town. Both men exited the Jeep. Holmes was impressed by the vast desert vista that lay before him. Such wide-open spaces must allow for a feeling of freedom one did not experience in the claustrophobia of the cities. The location was well-chosen. The two men might be seen, but they couldn't be heard.

Holmes quickly filled the young agent in on the details of the kidnapping without disclosing that Jenny Winston was in fact Agent Piper Sands.

"What do you want to know, Mr. Holmes? How can I help you?"

"Let's begin with how the Soviets communicate with you."

"Most often through an ordinary Post Office box in Roswell. Nothing bears a Russian postmark, of course. Anything coming directly from the Soviet Union is scrubbed in Seattle."

"Scrubbed?" Holmes asked.

"Repackaged, so the envelope bears a Seattle postmark."

"How do you communicate with them?"

"There is an old farm with several junk cars on it a few miles from Roswell. The trunk of one of the cars is a drop box. That is where I drop my regular reports. I drive to the farm and leave my package. I have never seen anyone at the farm. I assume it is a Soviet owned property."

"Might the girl be there?"

"Doubtful."

"The telephone number Colonel Hawker provided me with, do the Russians have it?"

"Yes, but we never speak over that telephone. That is only ever done through a pay telephone. The phone will ring and a voice at the other end will either speak the number one or thirty."

"What is the significance of that?"

"Time. Thirty means respond within thirty minutes. One means one hour. They allow for travel time to a phone booth."

"Thirty minutes would suggest a call of higher priority."

"Calls are rare, Mr. Holmes."

"If the need arises, are you able to initiate a call?"

"Yes, I have a telephone number. I call. Someone answers. I identify myself by repeating the banner headline of that day's *New York Times*. A few minutes later I get a call back. It is impossible to determine where the incoming call is coming from. The Soviets are thorough."

"Tell me about your predecessor."

"The former Comrade Cherepanov had gained access to a number of highly classified programs regarding aviation and technology. He had been copying documents and dropping them at the farm. From there, the agent who had recruited and groomed Cherepanov would pick up the documents and pass them on. The recruiter went by the name Smith. Like me, Cherepanov is American. He had never been to the Soviet Union, nor had he any contacts there. No one in Soviet intelligence has ever seen a photograph of Cherepanov. He was a name only. As he had been providing valuable intelligence, what did it matter if anyone had seen him? Everyone was happy. The Soviets had a well-oiled machine until Mr. Smith got drunk at a local bar, crashed his car, and ended up in intensive care. When the police investigated, they found copies of highly classified documents in the trunk of Smith's car. Intelligence was called in and Mr. Smith received a bedside visit. In his weakened condition, he gave up Cherepanov and numerous other details about his activities. As no one had ever seen Cherepanov, Central Intelligence plucked me from the ranks, and I took his place. Like Mr. Smith, Cherepanov was more than cooperative. He laid bare his soul. We knew the Soviet's would smell a rat if Smith simply disappeared. We made sure he notified the Soviets that he would require a lengthy period of bed rest once he was released from the hospital. To preserve my cover and prove my value to the state, I notified the Soviets that Smith had expressed reservations about continuing in his role. I added that I felt my own position was in jeopardy, that I had lost confidence in Smith. A few days later Mr. Smith passed away unexpectedly. Not long after I received a thank you card postmarked Seattle."

"Do you still use the farm to transmit reports and documents?"

"No. Apparently having someone pick up reports was viewed as a liability. Now I send them to a private box in Portland."

"What do you know about the Jenny Winston operation?"

"Hardly anything. From the moment the Roswell incident hit the newspapers, the Soviets wanted as much information as possible. I am still in the dark about Roswell."

"Why do you think the Soviets are so interested in Jenny Winston?"

"She was a witness to what happened. Supposedly she disappeared, or she was dead, and now she shows up in an Air Force newspaper. That's the kind of thing that gets the Soviets' attention."

"From the Soviet end, how involved were you?"

"Not very. My Moscow contact was the one to alert me to the Wright-Patterson photo. They pressed me hard, but I haven't been able to tell them anything."

"Do you know the name of your Moscow contact?"

"No. Names are never exchanged."

"Were you made aware of the operation to kidnap the girl?"

"Not specifically. I was told an operation involving the Winston girl was in the planning stages. No details were shared with me. I was told I would be notified when the operation would commence, and that didn't happen. The next thing I know, the operation has already been executed. Something changed."

"Is the girl still in the country.?"

"I cannot say for sure. My guess is yes. It seems unlikely she was ferreted out on a commercial flight. All airports and ports are on high alert. The Soviets would not risk flying a private plane across U.S. borders to Canada or Mexico. The plane most likely landed at a secluded airstrip."

"There must be thousands of places where a small plane can land."

"A needle in a haystack for sure."

"What about Cherepanov's house? How thorough was the search?"

"Intelligence crawled all over it."

"Is the house sealed?"

"Yes, it is in government possession."

"Can you take me there?"

"Of course, but I don't know what you expect to find. As I said, intelligence went over it in excruciating detail."

"I would like to see for myself."

"Very well. The house is in Roswell. It will take us about three hours."

"If something was missed, I will find it."

"I wouldn't count on it. Clean as a whistle. With all due respect, Mr. Holmes, you will not find anything of use. Intelligence is very thorough."

The hot and dusty drive in an open-air vehicle took every bit of three hours. Holmes was filthy with sweat and dust by the time he and Victor arrived at the tiny house that been the residence of the previous agent. Victor pulled a key from his pocket and let Sherlock Holmes inside.

Shut up as it had been, the house was stifling and muggy. The interior was a complete wreck. The entire place had been torn apart. The young agent told Holmes to take his time. He would be outside relaxing on the porch swing.

Holmes had to give the Americans credit. They had been thorough. Impressions were lifted from scratch pads, books opened, photo frames torn apart, the undersides and backs of furniture examined. Every inch had been put under the microscope. Holmes spent a good hour looking for clues a normal investigation would not reveal. Reluctantly he had to admit to himself there was

132

nothing. Perhaps if he had been allowed to investigate before the destruction began, he might have discovered a vital clue.

He cleared a spot on the settee and sat down. Staring at the empty book shelves opposite, he tried to imagine where an agent might conceal information he wished to keep hidden. The books scattered all over the living room floor suggested there was nothing to be found. With his foot, he sifted through the remnants of Cherepanov's library. The agent seemed not to have been interested in much other than cheap pulp fiction. Among the collection of potboilers, a familiar looking publication drew Holmes's attention. It was a road atlas like the one he had consulted in the Washington bookstore. He turned through the pages, imagining an American agent having done the same, pausing to read each note and scribble. Scribbled on the inside back cover were the following letters.

MEIINOh

Holmes was certain an agent had lingered over those letters for a long time before deciding they had no meaning in English or Russian. Yet one did not jot down meaningless letters. Were they a code? Why were all the letters written in capitals except the letter H? No, these were not random letters. They had meaning. This was a puzzle, but puzzles could only be solved if there were a frame of reference. One had to discover an association. He studied the letters for some time. Did they have something to do with a state? That seemed possible, but it was a guess at best. He laid the atlas on the settee and stood up. The room was filled with too much clutter to pace. He glanced at the letters again. Suddenly Holmes burst into laughter.

"Are you all right, Mr. Holmes?" Victor called to him from outside.

"No worries, old chap. Carry on."

The solution was so positively amateurish, Holmes could kick himself for overthinking it. One only had to view the letters upside-down to realize they were coordinates.

4ONII3W

The letters read 40 degrees north and 113 degrees west. Holmes exited onto the porch. "Do you have the tools necessary to plot coordinates?"

"Yes, in my Jeep. You found something?"

"Scribbled inside the back page of this atlas."

Victor retrieved the compass from his Jeep. He opened the atlas to the map of the entire United States. After a few quick calculations, Victor said, "Utah."

Holmes turned to the map of Utah.

Victor made another quick calculation. "The Great Salt Flats."

"A place where one could land a plane?" Holmes asked.

"It's a place where you can land hundreds of planes. It is west of Salt Lake City."

"Is Salt Lake the nearest major airport?"

"Yes, Salt Lake City Municipal. I watched intelligence go over every inch of this place. They looked through everything. I can't believe they missed this."

"It does seem unusual, doesn't it?" Holmes said.

"Maybe they thought the letters were worthless gibberish."

"Perhaps," Holmes mused. "Get me to a telephone as quickly as possible."

Victor drove Holmes to a local service station with a telephone booth outside.

"Get a message to Colonel Hawker. Have him send a detail to the Salt Lake City airport. That will likely be the arrival point of a Soviet agent known as The Caretaker. Passengers arriving with foreign passports should be given extra scrutiny. Any information you receive from the Soviets should be passed along to the Colonel without delay."

"Of course, but you shouldn't go this alone."

"I appreciate the offer, my young friend. Keeping you safe is paramount. We shouldn't risk any possibility of exposing you. You are much too important to the security of the nation."

Holmes waited until the young agent was out of sight before he entered the telephone booth. He pulled a small card from his pocket and dialed the operator. Moments later his call went through.

"Bob's Air Service," the voice on the other end of the line announced.

"This is Sherlock Holmes."

"Who?"

"I am a friend of Bob," Holmes said impatiently. "Have Bob meet me at the Roswell Airpark."

"Roswell, New Mexico?" The voice asked.

"Yes," Holmes snapped.

"Hell, mister, we're in Amarillo. That's 200 miles from here!"

"Bob assured me I could depend on him if there is anything I need. I require a flight to Utah."

"Bob isn't due in for another hour. I'll radio him. Maybe he can get there sooner."

"I will be waiting for him."

CHAPTER 20
After the fact

Kasputin Yar

Yuri Olenev pushed open the door of the hangar. A blast of cold air and snow blew inside. He pulled back the wolf rough of his parka and removed his snow goggles. Dmitri Sokolov was standing below the gleaming saucer, pretending to be interested in the work The Team was undertaking.

The young officer pulled his superior aside.

"Major, we have a matter we must discuss in private."

"Go up to my office. I will be there in a minute."

When Sokolov arrived, Yuri Olenev had removed his coat and poured two glasses of vodka.

"I took the liberty. I hope you don't mind."

Sokolov never minded a glass of vodka.

"Operation Minnie Mouse is over," Yuri said.

"Over? Were we not to be notified in advance?"

"That was my understanding."

"This information comes from Cherepanov?"

"A contact in Moscow. He has a friend close to Director Shubin."

"Say no more. We will leave well enough alone. Nothing good ever comes of a peeled onion."

"I suppose," Yuri said, not sure how to interpret Sokolov's aphorism.

"Has the operation succeeded? Do we have the girl?"

"Yes, but things did not go as planned. Sherlock Holmes and Dr. Watson were at the girl's house when our agents arrived."

"Holmes? What in hell was Holmes doing there?"

136

"That is what I do not know. One of our agents attempted to kidnap him."

Sokolov poured another drink. "What in holy hell is going on? Did the agent succeed?"

"No, Dr. Watson shot him."

"Watson killed a Soviet agent?"

"That came later. Dr. Watson wounded the man. Another of our agents put him out of our misery. He had become a liability."

"What about the girl? Where is she?"

"Unknown."

"Five years ago, Holmes and Watson were at the Roswell crash site, and now this. What are we to make of this, Yuri?"

"That is what I cannot understand. It seems unlikely they were at the girl's home by coincidence."

Sokolov filled both glasses again. "Either our operation was compromised, or this is the work of Shubin. My money is on Shubin. Have a plane readied. We are going to Moscow."

***

Moscow

"General-Major Sokolov and Lt. Olenev to see you, sir."

"Show them in." Director Shubin depressed the button on his intercom. This was not going to be a pleasant conversation.

Major Dmitri Sokolov and Lt. Yuri Olenev were shown into Director Shubin's office. Without looking up, Shubin gestured for the two men to sit.

"To what do I owe the pleasure, Major?"

"Operation Minnie Mouse."

"You are to be congratulated on a fine success, Major."

"Was it a success?" Sokolov asked.

"We have the girl."

"How did Sherlock Holmes become involved?"

"It is a long story."

"We have time."

"I saw an opportunity to kill two birds with one stone."

"Holmes was not a part of our operation."

"Your operation? All operations come through this office, Major. That means Moscow oversees all intelligence operations. Once an operation is approved, it is in our hands. We amend operations as we see fit. Am I clear?"

Rank forced Sokolov to exhibit the proper deference.

"I mean no disrespect, Chief Director. It seems to me as if the entire plan might have been put in jeopardy."

"And yet it wasn't. Our main objective was achieved. We have the girl. Holmes proved most useful. He led us to the girl sooner than we might otherwise have been able to grab her. Had we been able to grab Holmes as well, that would have been a bonus."

"What did you hope to gain by capturing Holmes?"

"Blackmail, leverage, humiliation. Revenge. We could have made the British look like fools."

"Forgive me, Chief Director. What do the British have to do with this?"

"It was personal!" Shubin said explosively, hammering his fist on the desk.

Sokolov and Yuri reflexively snapped back in their chairs. The small framed photograph tipped backwards onto the desktop. As a courtesy Sokolov leaned forward and returned the framed photo to its upright position, but not before noticing the familiar young woman framed against the Eiffel tower.

"Let me ask you this," Shubin continued. "Did you consider the girl might have been a trap? Did you not question why a photograph of someone given identity protection appeared in a military newspaper? No, you did not. It may well have been an operation designed to expose our network within the United States. Either way, it makes no difference because we have achieved our main objective. Leave the business of espionage to those who know something of it."

"Where is the girl now?"

"We have a safe facility near the Great Salt Flats in Utah. It is too risky to get her out of the country. We will get what we need from her. The Caretaker is on his way."

"What about Holmes?" Sokolov asked. "Where is he?"

"He has gone underground. We have lost him."

"And Dr. Watson?"

"He is still in Washington D.C. He is under continual surveillance." Shubin poured three glasses of Vodka. "Have a drink, Dmitri. After, go back to your toy box and do whatever it is you do there. When we have the information we need, we will pass it along."

Once on the street where they could not be overheard, Sokolov drew Yuri aside.

"It is now clear to me why Shubin wanted Holmes involved. The girl in the photograph on his desk was a British aerospace worker Shubin had an affair with several years ago. She was personally arrested by the brother of Sherlock Holmes. I was forced to listen to his story one night in a bar. He was drunk and weeping, carrying on like a schoolboy who has been rejected at a dance."

"Involving Holmes was personal."

"Stupid ass! He has jeopardized the entire operation over a woman. With Holmes in the picture, that means the British are now involved."

"Has the time come for Operation Dead Loop?" Yuri asked.

"Not yet. We will wait to see what The Caretaker learns."

CHAPTER 21
Dinner for two

Georgetown

Mycroft Holmes and I were scheduled to return to London on the same flight. As that would not occur until the following afternoon, I was pleasantly surprised to receive an invitation from Mycroft asking me to join him for dinner at an intimate little restaurant in Georgetown not far from my hotel. When I arrived by taxi, Mycroft was already seated.

A waiter brought a bottle of wine to the table.

"Something special. You don't mind, do you?"

"Of course not." Mycroft had exquisite taste. I had no doubt the wine would be superb. He asked if he could suggest our meal. I agreed, and we toasted good cheer. After a few minutes of requisite chitchat, I asked why he had invited me for dinner.

"As an expression of thanks. I want you to know how much I value your friendship with Sherlock, and how much I value your friendship."

"That is very kind of you, Mycroft. But seriously, what is the real purpose of this dinner?"

"I am afraid you have spent too much time in the company of my brother. Cynicism doesn't suit you." Mycroft refilled our glasses. "You have been a good friend to Sherlock. I say that with genuine sincerity. You will agree our meeting with Colonel Hawker was illuminating."

"Yes, if not unsettling."

"There is much you do not know to which you are entitled."

"Please, don't tell me Moriarty is back."

"No. Rest assured of that."

How many times had I heard that pronouncement over the years?

"You will recall the case of Ellen Sharpe."

"The woman convicted of passing to the Soviets highly classified documents related to the development of The Comet."

"We now know the name of her contact in Paris. Arkady Shubin. He is the Soviet director of foreign intelligence. I was the one who personally arrested Miss Sharpe."

"I fail to see the connection—" I reconsidered. "Oh, I see. Drawing Sherlock into the Jenny Winston affair was a revenge motive. Shubin was seeking revenge against you by kidnapping Sherlock."

"It seems the plausible explanation."

"You learned this how? Did Miss Sharpe have belated change of heart?"

"Initially, no. It seems we have an ally in the Kremlin. A photograph of Miss Sharpe was sent anonymously to our ambassador in Moscow. Across the photo was written *With Love, Arkady Shubin*."

"Someone else with a grudge, perhaps. Any clue as to the identity of the individual?"

"SIS is developing some ideas. Across the back of the photograph were scribbled the words *Women scorned*."

"Women, not woman?"

"Women."

"That narrows it down to half the population of the Soviet Union."

"One might conclude the sender felt she and Miss Sharpe were birds of a feather, so to speak. The photograph is a copy. The original appeared in *The Times of London* five years ago. One doesn't usually keep copies of past newspapers. That the individual was also able to make a high-resolution copy of Miss Sharpe's photo is telling. It might suggest the work of a Soviet analyst."

"Or a librarian."

"When confronted with the photograph, Miss Sharpe acknowledged she and Shubin had been lovers."

"If Miss Sharpe had been resolute for so long, what persuaded her?"

"We offered her a full pardon. Continuing to incarcerate Miss Sharpe no longer serves the interests of the crown."

"In other words, Miss Sharpe might prove more valuable outside of prison than in."

"John, you could have had a wonderful career as a civil servant."

"I prefer my role as doctor, writer, and companion to Sherlock Holmes. By the way, have you shared with Colonel Hawker that Shubin is the one who wanted Sherlock involved?"

"One doesn't share everything."

"Not even with friends?"

Mycroft chose not to answer my question.

Our meal arrived. As much as I did not wish to inflate Mycroft's ego more than necessary, his choice of restaurant, wine, and meal exceeded my expectations. Later we withdrew to an adjoining smoking room for brandy and cigars.

"While I am thoroughly enjoying the evening, I cannot help but note this is a very public setting for a man of your position."

Mycroft swilled his brandy. "Well observed. Visibility is the point of meeting in this delightful restaurant. Washington, as is London, is crawling with spies these days. We have watchers who are watching the watchers. The owners of this establishment love top government officials. All manner of spies come here for dinner. With their unlimited expense accounts, they buy the most expensive spirits and wines."

"Much was spoken of trust in our meeting with Colonel Hawker. Is your analyst in the Kremlin trustworthy?"

"She led us to the individual responsible for ensuring Sherlock's participation in the Jenny Winston affair. I neither trust her nor distrust her. She provided us with a useful piece of information. Where things go from here is entirely up to her."

"My sense is that you don't entirely trust the Americans."

Mycroft chuckled and poured us both more brandy. "Do you imagine the Americans are not spying on us?"

"Your response suggests they are."

"They are, indeed. There are no lines that cannot be crossed. They are spying on us; we are spying on them. You were correct in your observation during our meeting with Colonel Hawker that this game — this bloody game, I think you said — is risky. Lives are at stake, livelihoods, prosperity, safety, you name it."

"Then why play?"

"The alternative is war. We have no choice but to spy on our enemies and our allies alike. Alliances may change overnight. Information is the new currency. And friends are not always forthcoming. We share with the Americans only what serves our interests. In turn they provide us only with what they wish us to know."

"All seems a bit silly, if you ask me."

"Silly, but necessary, John. It is really a matter of simple economics. One must compete if one is to survive. In times of war our nation and our allies come together to form a formidable alliance. Off the field we compete against each other, not with. Each of us seeks an advantage over the other when it comes to trade, contracts, or international agreements. Intelligence is critical to achieving that advantage. If you and I play a game of cards, I have the advantage if I know what cards you are holding. Intelligence is the instrument that allows me to know your hand. Armed with that information, I know how far you can go."

"Are we stealing secrets from the Americans?"

"Espionage does not always involve absconding with blueprints in a briefcase. It is far more complex and subtle. Friendships are cultivated over time. Conversations over drinks are steered in certain directions. A home is searched while the occupant is away. Threats may be used to expose an infidelity. A lover might ask a favor."

"If Sherlock knew then what you are telling me now, I wonder if he might not have thought better of taking on this case?"

"Have you asked yourself why Sherlock acquiesced?"

"Admittedly I was surprised. Initially he seemed to have no interest."

"The day you spent with your editor revising your manuscript, Sherlock came to see me regarding Miss Ransom's visit. As you noted in our meeting with Colonel Hawker, Sherlock sensed something was amiss from the beginning. Never mind all that Jenny Winston was born in England palaver. The two men at the bus stop alerted Sherlock to the possibility there was more to Miss Ransom's request than merely locating Jenny Winston. For Colonel Hawker's benefit, it was necessary for Sherlock and me to play a little scene. He pretends he knows nothing; I pretend he is not as clever as he seems. This really was a matter for the Americans. The Soviets overplayed their hand."

"You believe Shubin's agents had been following Sherlock?"

"They were following Miss Ransom. They were present to confirm she contacted Sherlock."

"What is your interest in this matter?"

"Twofold. First, we have assets in place in America whose identities we wish to protect. The Jenny Winston affair would come dangerously close to exposing British operations in the U.S. As somebody obviously wanted Sherlock involved, we felt it best to see where this led."

"What is your second interest?"

"Roswell. We want to know the truth about the Roswell incident. The Americans won't share, and that upsets us, yet another justification for a British network in the U.S."

"Have you any idea what really happened out there?"

"We have lots of ideas. Some are simple, others are farfetched."

We sat for a moment, quietly staring into the fire, swilling our brandies.

"Is that everything?" I asked.

"John, it is never everything. Some things, however, are best left unsaid."

I raised my glass. "To things best left unsaid."

After finishing the evening with a cup of coffee, Mycroft offered to give me a lift to my hotel. I had a bit of a foggy head. I declined the offer of a lift, preferring instead to walk. The fresh air would do me good.

"Do you think that is wise, John? I cannot stress to you the need to be careful."

"I appreciate your concern. My hotel isn't far. I will be fine."

"Very well." Mycroft bid me good night and said he would see me after our return to London.

The night air was brisk and sobering. I established my bearings and set off for a leisurely stroll to the hotel. For no longer than I had been walking, I realized I had either misjudged the distance to the hotel or I had gotten lost. Admittedly I did not know Washington that well. Perhaps I had had more wine than I realized. I should return to the restaurant to call a taxi, I thought. As if my need had been anticipated, a yellow cab appeared, slowly creeping down the street toward me. Had it been following me? No doubt I stood out as a tourist thoroughly lost and in need of assistance. The taxi pulled up to the curb adjacent to the spot where I was standing. The driver gave me a friendly wave and switched off the for-hire sign on the roof. I hopped into the backseat.

"The Marquis Hotel," I said.

"You got it, Mister."

The driver set the meter and pulled into the sparse night traffic. After a couple of minutes, the driver glanced into the rearview mirror and said, "If you don't mind my saying, a gentleman such as yourself shouldn't be alone on the streets at night."

"Point well taken," I replied. "I thought I knew my way."

"Don't worry about a thing, you'll be taken good care of."

What a hectic three days it had been, I thought as my taxi wound its way through the streets of Washington to my hotel. The disastrous affair with Agent Sands, the meeting with Colonel Hawker, and dinner with Mycroft were almost too much to take in. I felt exhausted. Beginning with my meeting in London with my new editor Miss Terry, I had continually been reminded we now lived in a brave new world. This new world was a world of lies and mistrust. Mycroft and others seemed to navigate effortlessly through it, but I was not so eager to accept it. Perhaps that was why I enjoyed writing. It was the only place I could escape to where the world was that of my own creation.

I was so caught up in such ruminations, that I hadn't been paying attention to my journey. It seemed to me as if we had left Washington D.C. all together.

"I say," I said to the driver. "Are you sure this is the way to the Marquis?"

"I believe I missed a turn. I'll just pull over."

The taxi pulled to the roadside on a long, dimly lit street. No other cars were in sight. The driver rolled down his window and then bent over to reach for something. When he sat up and turned toward me, he was holding a handkerchief over his nose and mouth. With the other hand he was pointing something at me that looked like a pen.

"Don't worry," the man said. "It's just a little something to make you sleep."

Before I could cover my face, the driver's head snapped back, and he slumped over onto the passenger seat.

"You all right, Dr. Watson?" A man asked, pushing his head through the driver's side window.

"Yes, I think so, a bit shaken," I said.

"Let's get you back to your hotel," the unknown man said. He opened the rear door of the taxi and escorted me to another automobile parked behind.

"Nice to see you again, John," a voice said as I slid into the backseat of a black limousine.

"Good lord, Mycroft, what is going on?"

"Earlier when I said you really must be careful, I was not being polite. Whether here or in London, you are a target of the Soviets. You were lucky this time. Fortunately, my driver had observed the taxi before you exited the restaurant."

I had no words. All I could say was, "Thank you."

CHAPTER 22
The call

Early the next morning the telephone in my hotel room rang. It was the hotel operator. "Dr. Watson, I have a long-distance call for you from New York. Will you take the call?"

I couldn't imagine why anyone from New York was calling me, but I took the call, in case it was Holmes. Why he would be in New York, I had no idea.

"Hello?"

"Dr. Watson?"

The voice sounded emotionally flat, but familiar. I couldn't place it.

"It's Miss Terry."

"Eden?" I asked, unable to conceal the surprise in my voice. *Dr. Watson? Miss Terry?* Hadn't we parted company in London on a first name basis?

"Yes. I am in New York. I wonder if you could meet me here."

"New York?"

"Yes, I am meeting with our American publisher."

"Forgive me. How did you know I was in America?"

"Oh!" There was a long pause. "Mrs. Portland. I contacted your housekeeper."

The tenor of our conversation felt off.

"Go on."

"I have some issues I need to go over with you. If you could meet me at my hotel."

"Your timing is fortuitous. I will be leaving Washington for New York within the hour. I am not sure how much time I will have in New York."

"It is very important, Doctor. Most important."

"I take you at your word."

"When you arrive at my suite, don't bother knocking. The door will be unlocked. I will be waiting for you."

Miss Terry provided me with the name of her hotel and room number.

After putting down the phone, I realized I had broken into a sweat. There was something odd about Miss Terry's tone, and yet this unexpected and odd invitation felt vaguely seductive.

"Silly old man," I said to myself.

***

New York City

It turned out my layover in New York allowed ample time to take a taxi into the city and address the issues Miss Terry had raised on the telephone. I entered the hotel lobby and took a lift to the tenth floor. When I arrived at room 1001, my first impulse was to knock, but she had said to come in without knocking.

I swung the door open. "Hello?" There was no answer. "Hello? Miss Terry? It's me, John Watson." Still no answer.

The room was a suite. Slowly I walked through the hallway to a sitting room. To my utter shock, there in the middle of the room was Eden Terry, tied to a chair, wearing nothing but her underclothes. Her head was slumped forward. Clearly, she was unconscious. I rushed to her side and knelt before her.

"How nice of you to come Doctor, to rescue your damsel in distress."

I looked up. A man with a Russian accent had entered from an adjoining room.

151

"What's going on here?" I demanded. "What have you done to her?" I pulled off my coat and wrapped it around Miss Terry.

"Ah, yes. The English. Such gentlemen."

"I said, what have you done to her?"

"Not to worry, just a mild sedative. She will awake thoroughly refreshed and not remember a thing."

"Where are her clothes? What kind of animal are you?"

"Doctor, a veteran such as yourself, you know we all employ various methods of persuasion."

"Whatever it is you want this woman knows nothing."

"Quite right. She is the cheese to entice the mouse."

"And you will get nothing from me."

"I doubt that, Doctor. Once you meet The Caretaker, I believe you will give him everything he needs."

Someone moved behind me. Before I could turn around, I felt a slight prick in the neck. In an instant, I was out.

CHAPTER 23
The Caretaker

The Great Salt Flats

The agents Piper Sands referred to as Moe and Larry sat at a small table in the upper hangar playing cards. With little else to do until The Caretaker arrived, playing cards had become their routine. Their prisoners were well-secured. They had plenty of time to waste and plenty of time to think. Neither agent felt valued. Life as a secret Soviet agent had far less glamour than had been presented at the academy. They were little more than thugs.

The sound of a plane circling overhead announced the arrival of The Caretaker. The agents put away their cards and went outside to meet the plane.

Moe reached inside his jacket and pulled a pistol from its holster. He checked to make sure he had a fully loaded clip.

"Put that away," Larry said.

"Do you know The Caretaker?" Moe asked.

"By reputation only."

"Neither do I. Best to be safe."

Following his partner's lead, Larry patted the bulge beneath his left armpit.

The twin-engine plane touched down on the white sand runway and taxied slowly toward the hangar. After the props stopped spinning, a tall man carrying a black medical bag exited the plane. The pilot remained onboard.

The Caretaker approached. Both agents felt a moment of trepidation. The Caretaker's hair was parted in the middle, he had a pencil thin moustache, wore steel rimmed glasses, and he had a scar that ran from the length of his left eye to the corner of his mouth. His appearance was every bit as unsettling as his reputation.

"Comrade, it is a pleasure to welcome you," Moe said. "I am Agent Mikhail Lebedev, and this is my colleague Agent Alexei Egorov."

The Caretaker halted before the two agents. He studied their faces carefully, as if his eyes were X rays.

"I have little time. Take me to the prisoner."

For a Russian, Moe thought to himself, The Caretaker had an excellent command of English. In the academy, agents in training had been taught to take nothing for granted.

"Ваш английский отличный, товарищ," Moe said.

"It is not necessary to test me, Agent Lebedev. I speak seven languages without a hint of my native tongue. Shall we proceed?"

"Of course. This way."

The two agents led The Caretaker downstairs to the cells below the hangar.

"The girl is here," Larry said. He unlocked the cell door while Moe stepped back, pistol in hand.

Piper Sands was seated on a settee, reading the only book available to her, *War and Peace.*

When Piper Sands looked up into the face of the stranger, she did a double take and burst out laughing. "Are you kidding me?"

Moe and Larry glanced at each other nervously. Such impertinence, such disrespect.

"Quiet!" Moe demanded. "This is The Caretaker!"

"This is your scary Caretaker? He looks like an escapee from a Nazi melodrama."

Larry stepped forward to silence the prisoner.

The Caretaker raised his hand. "Leave us. Shut the door, but do not lock it."

"Are you certain, Comrade?"

"Do as I say. I will take care of this impertinent young woman. Get out!"

Both agents stepped out of the room and closed the door behind them.

Piper Sands exhaled a deep breath. "Am I glad to see you."

Sherlock Holmes removed the steel rimmed glasses. "I can hardly see with these things."

"I am sorry, I almost blew your cover. I wasn't sure what to expect. I just wasn't expecting you. You have a habit of showing up at the most unexpected times."

"I apologize for the cheap theatrics. Tucumcari has little in the way of theatrical supplies. Apparently, that pair of thugs was convinced, and that's all that matters. Now, we must act quickly. I have no idea how much time we have or how much longer I can maintain this charade."

"What do you want me to do?"

"I have syringes in this bag. Once I open the door, you will need to appear as if I have sedated you. I will invite our friends inside to move you. You will have one syringe hidden at your side, and I will hold the other at my side. You will inject one; I will inject the other."

"That seems easy enough."

As an afterthought, Holmes added, "You should probably scream."

"Naturally, isn't that what all helpless women do?"

"I mean no disrespect. We are improvising. As a reminder, I have no idea how much time we have."

"What about the prisoner next door?"

"There is another captive?"

"Brought in early this morning. I heard the banging on the door and walls. It's impossible to know who it is."

"Whomever, we shall soon find out."

As instructed, Piper Sands gave several mighty screams and then reclined quietly on the settee, the syringe hidden at her side.

Holmes opened the door of the cell.

"Take her. I have what I need. Get rid of her."

Moe and Larry entered the room. Moe gently leaned over the lifeless body of the prisoner while Larry stood behind him. As Moe bent near, Piper Sands opened her eyes. Moe jumped back, recoiling at the sudden stab in his arm. At the same instant, Larry also recoiled, suddenly aware of a sharp pain in his neck. Seconds later both men collapsed onto the floor.

Holmes pointed to Larry. "This one has the keys."

Piper Sands knelt over the fallen agent she called Larry. She removed a set of keys from the agent's pocket. Quickly she and Holmes went to the next cell and threw open the door.

"Watson?" Holmes said with utter surprise.

"Holmes?" I cried with equal astonishment. His preposterous disguise was jarring.

"Doctor?" Agent Sands blurted out.

"Holmes, I thought I'd never—"

"No time to talk old chap, we must leave now. I am afraid we may be on borrowed time. I have a plane waiting."

Agent Sands, Holmes, and I fled to the upper part of the hangar. We dashed outside only to stop abruptly. Another plane was parked nearby. Two henchman holding pistols and a small framed man with a medical bag were waiting for us. Several yards further on was another plane, only this one was on fire. I assumed it must have been the plane Holmes flew in on. Whatever the fate of the pilot, I had no idea. I hated to think he was inside the burning plane.

"Sherlock Holmes, so nice to meet you at last. General Leonid Lukin, at your service."

"You will forgive me if I fail to appreciate the moment."

General Lukin chuckled and shook his head. "The English sense of humor. Your disguise. Is this how the British imagine Soviet operatives?"

"What did I tell you?" Agent Sands said. "Good lord, get rid of that ridiculous scar and creepy moustache."

"It was a matter of expedience," Holmes said, removing his disguise.

"Time! There never seems to be enough. There is so much to talk about Mr. Holmes, but I am afraid it is just not possible. Sadly, we will not have that opportunity."

Lukin snapped his fingers. One of the henchmen moved toward Piper Sands.

"Take me," Holmes said. "The girl knows nothing."

"You are mistaken, Mr. Holmes. It is you who knows nothing."

"Then take both of us," I said.

"Twice nothing is nothing, Doctor."

"From the beginning I have been a target," Holmes said.

"Your deaths combined with your complicity in the abduction of Miss Winston by unknown foreign agents will prove most scandalous."

The henchman grabbed a kicking and screaming Piper Sands and dragged her onto the plane. The young woman was no match for the brute manhandling her.

After the thug had bound and gagged his prisoner, he emerged from the plane and joined his fellow thug on the runway.

"Where is the pilot of the plane you arrived in, Mr. Holmes?"

Holmes glanced at the burning plane.

"I am an experienced pilot, General."

Lukin's expression suggested he was not convinced

"No matter. You have wasted my time Mr. Holmes and exhausted my patience." He turned to his henchmen. "Take them inside and lock them up. Then torch the entire facility."

With pistols in hand, the henchmen gestured for Holmes and me to re-enter the hangar.

"One last thing, General. How did you avoid being apprehended in Salt Lake City?"

"Cherepanov. He is our man, Mr. Holmes, not yours."

Lukin's thugs pushed us inside and down the stairs, locking us inside the cell where our former guards were still unconscious. Within minutes smoke began to drift in under the cell door.

Immediately Holmes and I set about reviving the sleeping agents. Any chance we might have of breaking down the door would require the strength of as many men as possible.

Even with the help of the groggy agents, the steel door would not budge. The heat on the other side of the door was beginning to raise the temperature in the cell.

"Holmes, this could be it," I said.

"I am afraid you are right, old chap."

The two Soviet agents kept smashing futilely against the door.

At the point I did not think I could remain conscious a second longer, the steel door swung open.

"Bob!" Holmes called out.

"Hurry, Mr. Holmes!" Our rescuer said. "The whole building could come down any moment."

As we reached the top of the stairs, the entire hangar was ablaze. Flaming insulation was falling from the ceiling and dropping onto the plane parked inside the hangar.

"We've got to save this plane," Bob yelled.

Immediately the grizzled old pilot hopped up onto the wing and got into the pilot's seat. For what seemed an interminably long time, the engines slowly cranked before catching and roaring to life.

Revving the engines, Bob steered the plane outside before the hangar completely collapsed. Once clear of the burning hangar, Bob gunned the engines and raced down the runway as if to take off. Instantly the flaming debris that had fallen onto the wings and fuselage blew away. Other than scorched paint, the plane was undamaged. Returning to the site of the burning hangar, Bob shut off the engines and exited the plane. "That was close," he said, hopping down from the wing.

"Jolly good show." I grabbed Bob's hand and introduced myself.

"How did you manage to avoid The Caretaker?" Holmes asked.

"Listening to your story about him while you put on your disguise, I guessed that fellow was a nasty character. When I saw his plane pass overhead for a landing, I slipped out of my own plane and hid myself just in case it was him. It looks as if I was right. He owes me a plane."

"And we owe you our lives," I said.

"Indeed," Holmes said. "Have you a way to track The Caretaker's plane?"

"This plane is not equipped for that."

"Then I am afraid we have lost the girl again."

"I think I might be able to help," Agent Alexei Egorov said.

"Don't be stupid, Alexei," his companion snapped. "These men are the enemy."

Alexei turned to Mikhail Lebedev. "The girl called us Moe and Larry. Do you know who Moe and Larry are?"

Lebedev shrugged his shoulders.

"They are part of an American comedy act called The Three Stooges. They are stooges because they are stupid. They are fools. You can continue to be Moe, but I will not be stupid or a stooge for you or the Soviet Union. Lukin left us to die in that hangar. These men, this enemy, saved our lives. I will take my chance."

"What can you tell us?" Holmes asked.

Egorov pulled a small notepad from inside his jacket and scribbled down a telephone number. "I cannot say for certain if this contact can help you, but it is worth a try. It has been a couple of years. I do not remember the last name. Ask for James. Something along those lines."

"Thank you," Holmes said.

"What happens to us?" Agent Lebedev asked.

"Dr. Watson and I are not Americans," Holmes replied. "We have no authority to take you into custody. I am afraid you are on your own."

"Then we will take our chances. Thank you, Mr. Holmes."

With Bob in the pilot's seat, ten minutes later we were airborne.

"Cherepanov," Holmes said. "Quite clever. Drawing my attention with an identical copy of the road atlas I consulted in the Washington D.C. bookstore. Obviously, I underestimated their surveillance methods. The Americans would never have overlooked a critical piece of information. It was Cherepanov who wrote those coordinates."

"Why go to that much trouble? Why not tell you the location instead of leaving the discovery to chance?"

"Telling me the location of a Soviet safe house would arouse my suspicions. It would have been too convenient. He would have been obligated to share that information with Intelligence and Colonel Hawker. Letting me discover it on my own keeps his cover safe."

"Hawker provided you with Cherepanov's contact number. All along I have had my doubts about that man."

"I know you have, old chap. It is unclear who we may trust."

After describing to Holmes what had happened to me in Washington and New York, I fell into a deep sleep, lulled into slumber by the hum of the engines.

CHAPTER 24
For every action

Kasputin Yar

Yuri Olenev put down the telephone. He was seated in his small office located a few hundred yards from the massive complex that housed The Olympus Project. Shakily he poured himself a drink. He felt as if he had been punched in the gut. For ten minutes he stared blankly through the window. "Good God," he said to himself. "Why did I ever become involved in this?"

He picked up the telephone and called the Major.

"How important?" The Major asked disagreeably.

"Urgent," Yuri responded.

Yuri Olenev slipped into his winter coat and walked across the way to the Major's office inside the hangar that housed The Olympus Project.

"Leave the door open," Major Sokolov said, "It is stuffy in here."

The junior officer removed his coat and shut the door.

Sokolov glanced up from his desk. He sighed and shook his head. "Yuri, will you ever bring me good news? What has happened now?"

"The safe house in Utah has been destroyed. The agents assigned to the Winston girl have disappeared. No word on the girl. The Caretaker may have been exposed. Sherlock Holmes and Dr. Watson are missing."

Sokolov smiled to himself and poured himself a strong, dark coffee. He offered a coffee to Yuri Olenev.

The young officer shook his head. "There is one more thing."

"One more thing?" Sokolov laughed. "Is it not enough Shubin's operation has apparently gone to hell?"

162

"I have additional information."

"From Cherepanov?"

"No, Cherepanov has gone silent. He may well be compromised." Yuri paused, still reeling from what he had learned. "This information comes from my source deep inside."

"Yes, yes. I am well-aware of your deep source contact. Get on with it."

"The girl. It turns out she is not Jenny Winston. She is an imposter. A plant. An American agent. She was not at Roswell. She knows nothing about the FD3. She was sent under cover to expose our network."

Sokolov switched from coffee to vodka. He poured a drink for himself and another for Yuri. "A toast, Yuri. To the Americans. They have played this brilliantly. First worthless blueprints, and now this. We have been chasing a ghost."

"Might not this girl, this agent, have some value to us? A bargaining chip perhaps?"

"No, Yuri, her job was to expose our operatives. Beyond that, her value to the Americans is that she knows nothing about Roswell. To them she is expendable; to us she is a waste of our time. We must take the current, Yuri."

Yuri Olenev gulped down his drink and poured another without asking his superior's permission. Sokolov was quoting Shakespeare. It was one thing to plot and plan a seemingly impossible if not ridiculous operation, but to give it a go, the implications were overwhelming. Should Operation Dead Loop fail, it would be impossible to calculate the fallout. He wished he could distance himself from this harebrained plan.

"Make the contact, Yuri. Operation Dead Loop is a go."

Roswell

Colonel Jim Patterson pushed open the folding door of the telephone booth. He had slammed down the receiver so hard, the phone's bell was still echoing as he stepped outside. He drew a deep breath and leaned against the fender of his car. His head was filled with conflicting thoughts. As an officer in the Air Force his job was to defend his country and the constitution. For four years he had been blackmailed by the Soviets who had threatened to expose his affair with Charlene. He should have called their bluff. Instead he had allowed himself to commit treason. Just one more time. It was always one more time. And now he had given them the most sensitive secret of all.

A shabby looking bar was directly across the road. He dodged a few oncoming cars and spent the rest of his afternoon trying to drink away his regrets.

Later at home he explained to his wife that he had had a hard day. Usually he worked out his troubles on the basketball court, his wife reminded him. Jim Patterson replied that his day had been exceptionally trying.

Salt Lake City

After saying farewell to Bob at a local small plane airpark, Holmes and I checked into a motel. My cell beneath the hangar had been better appointed.

"It won't be long," Holmes said. "Perhaps not even for the night."

Holmes dialed the telephone number the Soviet agent had given him. After three rings, a woman answered.

"Hello, Charlene's Beauty Salon. This is Charlene."

"I beg your pardon," Holmes said. "I must have telephoned the wrong number."

"Say," Charlene said. "Are you English? You sound English. Now what is an Englishman doing calling my beauty salon?"

"I am attempting to reach a gentleman by the name of James. My apologies."

"James? Do you mean Jim? If it's the Jim I know, Jim Patterson, he ain't no gentleman. But he sure is fun."

"Jim Patterson! Yes, Jim Patterson," Holmes said, recalling the Colonel we had met five years earlier. He had been an officer in what was then known as the Army Air Forces. "Is Jim there now? May I speak with him?"

"Oh, lord no. Jim is in New Mexico. This here is Texas, honey."

"Can you tell me how to reach Jim? Do you have a number for him?"

"I can't do that. Jim is pretty sensitive about that sort of thing."

"Madame—"

"Please, call me Charlene."

"Charlene, this is a matter of extreme urgency. If you could give me Jim's telephone number."

"Darling, I'd love to do that. You sound really cute and all with that England accent, but I just can't."

"Can you have him call me? It is a matter of national security."

"You sound awfully convincing. All right, I'll do that. Give me your telephone number."

Holmes reeled off the telephone number and room extension.

"What name should I give?"

"Sherlock Holmes."

"You are not!" Charlene gasped.

"I can assure you this is no joke."

"Is Dr. Watson with you?"

"Speak into the phone, Watson. Say hello to Charlene."

"Hello, Charlene. Nice speaking with you."

Charlene squealed so loudly Holmes had to move the receiver away from his ear.

"Charlene, it is most important that we hear from Jim as soon as possible."

"Oh my god!" Charlene warbled. "I'll call him right away."

After Charlene hung up the telephone, Holmes wiped his brow.

"Good lord, Holmes, is Colonel Patterson working for the Soviets? I think we have stumbled into a nest of vipers."

"We shall see. All we can do now is wait and hope Colonel Patterson calls."

Tooele, Utah

Wes Reed received the three successive calls shortly before dinner time.

First call, one ring; second call, two rings; third call, three rings. He had trained himself never to pick up a telephone before the first ring ended. Thirty seconds later the phone rang again. This time Reed picked up. A voice at the end spoke a telephone number. It was only stated once. Reed had fifteen minutes to get to a pay phone. Calls were rare, and they always signified something important. On his drive to find a pay phone, Reed wondered what would happen if another caller happened to call between rings or the minute in between the first series of calls. It hadn't happened yet, but you never knew.

Three miles from his home he used a pay phone outside of a drive-in restaurant. The drive-in was filled with teenagers in souped-up cars. He dialed the telephone number from memory. He assumed the number he was calling was also that of a pay phone. The phone at the other end picked up, but no one spoke.

"Rain is in the forecast," Reed said. It was a perfectly pointless phrase, but one deemed necessary for security and authentication.

"The operation is a go. Two nights from now," the voice on the other end of the line said. "I repeat, Dead Loop is a go."

The call disconnected.

Reed lit a cigarette. "Hmm," he said to himself. The voice at the other end of the line was American. Texan, Reed guessed. He chuckled. Had he been expecting a Russian?

Brownville, Texas

Charlene knew she shouldn't call Jim at home, but she had spoken with Sherlock Holmes and Dr. Watson, and, well, that seemed important.

After four rings, the phone picked up. "Hello?" The voice at the other end said.

"Damn!" Charlene said to herself. It was Jim's wife. What now?

"Hello? Hello?"

"Er, hello. May I speak with Jim—Colonel Patterson, please?"

"May I ask who is calling?"

"Er, Margie. I am calling from the base."

"Just a minute please."

A moment later Jim Patterson picked up the phone.

167

"Jim, it's me, Charlene."

Patterson almost dropped the receiver. He looked about to make sure his wife was out of the room. "Charlene, what are you doing? Are you crazy? You know you're never supposed to call me here."

"I know, Jim. I'm sorry, but it's urgent."

A dozen thoughts quickly ran through Jim Patterson's mind. What could be so urgent that Charlene had to call him at home?

"What's going on, Charlene?"

"Sherlock Holmes called me."

"Charlene, this isn't funny. I don't appreciate your calling me at home."

"This isn't a joke," Charlene bristled. "Why he called me, why he had my telephone number, I don't know. All I can tell you is he said it was urgent. He left a telephone number and said he hoped you would call him. That's it. Goodbye, Jim."

"Charlene, wait!"

The line went dead.

Jim's wife came back into the room. "What was that about?" She asked.

"Something has come up at the base. I'll be back shortly."

"What about your dinner?"

"Keep it warm. This won't take long."

Moscow

Arkady Shubin was awakened in the middle of the night.

"Good God," he barked into the telephone. "Have you any idea what time it is?"

"Apologies, Comrade Director, we have just received an important communique from our agents assigned to monitor telephone calls in America. It concerns the American, Colonel Patterson stationed in Roswell. Sherlock Holmes placed a call to Patterson's mistress in Texas."

"Holmes?" Shubin threw off the covers and sat on the edge of his bed. "Go on."

"He said it was important he speak with Colonel Patterson right away. It was a matter of extreme urgency."

"What else?"

"That was all. A few minutes later the woman called Patterson to relay the message."

"Nothing about what this urgent situation is?"

"Nothing!"

Shubin hung up the phone, slipped into his robe, and went into the kitchen. He sat at the table and lit a cigarette. So, Holmes was alive. The Caretaker had reported Holmes had been taken care of. And now this. What did Holmes want of Patterson? No doubt Holmes was on the trail of the girl, but how did Patterson fit into this picture?

Roswell

Jim Patterson drove out of town to make his call.

"Mr. Holmes?"

"Speaking."

"This is Colonel Jim Patterson. We met several years ago in Las Vegas."

"Colonel, thank you for returning my call. I do not have time to go into the details. An American agent by the name of Piper Sands has been abducted by the Soviets and I fear she is in great danger."

"Go on."

169

"Can you help me find Agent Sands? The men who have taken her hostage flew from the Salt Flats yesterday. I assume they are headed for a safe location. Do you know where?"

"Mr. Holmes, what makes you think I would know that information?"

"Colonel, the telephone number I was given was provided by a cooperative Soviet agent. It is not difficult to imagine why a beauty salon operator in a small Texas town would have the telephone number of an Air Force colonel in New Mexico. Need I say more?"

Patterson did not respond.

"A life is at stake here. When the Soviets discover the young woman cannot provide the information they are seeking, they will most certainly eliminate her."

Jim Patterson knew he had no choice.

"Very well, Mr. Holmes. Write down the following coordinates."

Holmes quickly jotted down the information provided by Colonel Patterson.

"Be at this exact location at 6 p.m. the day after tomorrow."

"Go on!"

"That's it. You have it. More than that I cannot say."

"Colonel, you have provided me with nothing but a location on a map. Will the girl be at this location?"

"I can't say. Perhaps. I have no way of knowing."

"Colonel, I cannot imagine the purpose of your game."

"Mr. Holmes, I assure you I am not playing a game. I have already put both my career and my marriage at risk. How you proceed will likely determine my future. You have no choice but to trust me."

The line went dead.

Jim Patterson felt both unburdened and uncertain. He was tired of living a lie and tired of being manipulated by the Soviets. This evening, he would have dinner with his wife, confess everything, and beg forgiveness. Whatever happened next would be entirely up to Sherlock Holmes.

Salt Lake City

"That seems not to have gone well," I remarked after Holmes rang off.

"The Colonel has given us very little to go on. We will need a map."

Twenty minutes later Holmes stabbed his finger onto a map we had appropriated from the motel manager.

"There! Pyrite Lake, New Mexico."

"Good God, Holmes. It is in the middle of nowhere. If the Colonel cannot be sure the girl is there, might we not be on a wild goose chase?"

"Indeed, but as the Colonel said, we have no choice but to trust him."

"From the moment we accepted this case, we have been lied to. Trust is a commodity in very short supply."

"By my calculations, Pyrite Lake is 410 miles from Salt Lake City. I believe our best course is to drive. We will hire a car tomorrow morning."

"In that case, I am going to pour myself a brandy and go to bed."

CHAPTER 25
Closing in

Before dawn Holmes and I were up and on our way from Salt Lake City, Utah to Pyrite Lake, New Mexico. The clerk at the auto hire agency wanted to know when we would return the vehicle. As we could not determine how long we would be engaged, we said a week. As for a local address, we provided the name and telephone number of the local motel in which we had been staying. With map in hand, we hunkered down for a long journey. We would alternate drivers every two hours. I volunteered to take the first shift.

"Holmes, don't you think there's a certain element of folly involved in this journey. We have no idea what we are headed into, what to expect."

"No question, old chap."

"We are depending on the good faith of Colonel Patterson, a man clearly of compromised integrity."

"I quite agree. We have been lied to, misdirected, and manipulated from the outset. Dark forces are at play, yet we cannot abandon our faith in humanity."

"Holmes, you sound like a man of the cloth. Such stirring sentiments. One could almost believe one is in chapel."

"What have we left, Watson, if we cannot continue to believe in fundamental decency?"

"That seems to be more of a challenge by the day."

"I cannot state with a certainty that Colonel Patterson is trustworthy; I pray my instincts will not fail me."

A vast stretch of deserted highway lay ahead of us. I hoped Holmes was right.

***

After several stops for petrol and refreshments, we arrived at Pyrite Lake eleven hours later. From the nearest main road, the lake was located almost ten miles in, accessible only by dirt road. The remaining half mile to the lake could only be traversed by foot along a rarely used path. The lake itself was hidden deep in the woods. According to a brochure we acquired at a petrol station, Pyrite Lake had been created millions of years ago by a giant meteor that had crashed to earth. Due to the arduous task of getting to the lake, few visitors made the trek in. Once we had punched through the dense brush growing over the footpath, we entered onto the lake itself surrounded by trees, save for an open area along the western shoreline farthest from our location. The open area was a curiously large clearing, noticeably absent of the trees lining the rest of the lake. Holmes removed a pair of field glasses from the knapsack he was carrying. After a moment, he handed the binoculars to me. While mostly green in appearance, the clearing showed signs of scorching, as if a fire had recently occurred there.

"What do you make of it?" I asked.

"A major fire would have blackened the entire area. From all indications, the scorching appears to have been made by several smaller fires."

"Campfires perhaps?"

"Inconclusive."

"To the matter at hand, where precisely are we to meet whomever or whatever for our six o'clock rendezvous tomorrow night? Here? The end of the road we drove in on? Or the clearing?"

The wind lifted and blew our direction. Holmes sniffed the air. "Do you smell that?"

"No, I smell nothing."

"A smoky smell."

"I see no smoke."

"The smell of something recently burned. It is drifting from the clearing."

"From the scorched spots, of course."

"An old fire would not continue to give off a burnt smell. No, Watson, those fires were recent. A week old at the most."

"Our meeting place will be the clearing based upon a smoky smell?"

Holmes turned to me and lifted his eyebrows.

"No," I stammered. "I do not have a better suggestion."

"The clearing," said Holmes. "We shall return tomorrow evening."

***

Holmes and I spent the night and following day in Aztec, New Mexico. He spent most of his day at the local library, while I toured the town and took in the tourist sites. Later that afternoon we took a late lunch at a local café and then set off again for Pyrite Lake. We arrived at the clearing shortly after 5 p.m. We wished to allow plenty of time to survey the surroundings and note the presence of others who might be anticipating our arrival. Unsure of what to expect, we took up a position well away from the clearing.

Dusk had already settled in when the first sign of something about to happen occurred. First came the hum of a craft coming near, followed seconds later by a large disc hovering above the clearing. It was as if a huge storm cloud were moving overhead.

"Good God, Holmes, what is that? Is that what Colonel Patterson sent us here to meet?"

"We are about to find out."

The disc began descending slowly. Approximately twenty feet above the ground, the craft hissed, and four struts appeared from small panels below the belly of the craft. The disc touched down. Lights from the perimeter of the ship illuminated the surrounding area. Another panel opened. This time a staircase slowly slid to the ground. Light from the interior of the craft illuminated the stairs and the ground immediately below. Two shadows projected onto the staircase from the interior lights of the craft. Occupants were about to disembark.

I glanced at Holmes. He raised a finger to keep quiet.

It was all I could do not to gasp. Two figures emerged, unlike any beings I had seen before. They were green with disproportionately large eyes. The pair of creatures descended the steps, entered onto the ground and began examining the exterior of the craft. Holmes and I watched with fascination. I could almost have convinced myself we were hallucinating. After concluding their inspection, the creatures moved away from the ship into the clearing. The lights from the ship provided enough illumination to observe the actions of the creatures. One reached into what I presumed to be a flap or fold in his skin and produced a small packet.

I elbowed Holmes. "What do you think they are doing?" I whispered.

Holmes pressed the field glasses to his eyes.

"Unless I am mistaken, I believe they are about to smoke a cigarette."

"What?"

Holmes handed the glasses to me.

"Good lord! Smoking a cigarette? What creatures are these?"

"Watson, we must get aboard that ship."

"Holmes, have you taken leave of your senses?"

"Colonel Patterson directed us here for a reason. Miss Sands may well be on board."

"Aside from the absurdity of such a suggestion, how can we manage that?"

"We create a distraction."

"Such as? Throwing a stone into the bushes and hoping they will investigate instead of returning to their ship?"

"Never mind, it appears that won't be necessary."

One of the creatures appeared to say something to the other. Both flicked away the remains of their cigarettes and disappeared into a clump of trees.

"This is our chance, Watson. Now!"

Holmes leaped from our hiding place and raced toward the ship. I had no time to consider our position and fell in behind. We raced up the stairway into the interior of the ship.

"Holmes, might there not be other creatures on board?"

"We shall find out. We must act quickly."

The interior of the craft was organized like a honeycomb containing a series of small compartments with sliding doors. Inside each compartment were flight seats and safety harnesses. The bridge that housed the pilot's controls was empty. Holmes and I made a quick search of the compartments. Piper Sands was not on board. At the point we were about to disembark, we heard movement on the stairs below. Holmes and I retreated to a cubicle, cracking the door enough to provide a view of the stairway. A single creature came up the steps and depressed a button which retracted the stairs. Immediately he went to the bridge.

"We need to get off now!" Holmes said.

We made our way to the exit stairs. Before we could press the button to engage the stairs, the ship's engines whined, and the craft slowly lifted. The landing struts hissed and retracted into the belly of the ship. The gravitational force was almost too much to bear. Holmes and I were practically paralyzed for what seemed an eternity. Within minutes the ship reached altitude and the environment within the saucer became stable, allowing us to move freely and to plot our move.

"Watson, are you all right?"

"Don't worry about me, what about you?"

"We are no worse for wear."

"What about the other pilot? Where is he? What happened?" I asked.

"It is pointless to speculate."

"Aren't two pilots necessary to operate this ship?"

"Clearly not, which may well be to our advantage. We need not worry about an extra crew member moving about the ship."

Now that the nervous excitement of the moment brought on by a burst of adrenaline had passed, the reality of what we had done was sinking in.

"Holmes, do you realize what we have done? We may be on a trip to outer space, another planet, or another galaxy. We may never see Earth again."

"Somehow, Watson, that is not my sense."

CHAPTER 26
A face in the clouds

Buffalo Gap, South Dakota

After two days of being locked away, Piper Sands finally saw daylight. She had been blindfolded and brought by car to a makeshift runway in the middle of nowhere. Her guards removed the blindfold and shackles. The spot was safe. There was nowhere to run, nowhere to hide. It was late evening; the sun was going down.

The Caretaker sat in the front passenger seat with the door open.

"Where are we?" Piper Sands asked.

The two Soviet agents assigned to guard the young woman ignored her question.

"Where are we!" She demanded again.

"Buffalo Gap, South Dakota," The Caretaker said.

"What are we doing here?"

"Waiting."

"Waiting for what?"

Piper Sands knew her chances of escape were minimal. Her training had stressed that asking questions was important. The more she could get from her captors, the more she had to work with, anything that might prove an advantage.

"We are waiting for a ride. Now be quiet, otherwise you will be bound and gagged. What is it you Americans say? Put a sock in it!"

Piper Sands decided it was best to keep her mouth shut. Being bound and gagged would do her no good.

Three quarters of an hour later, a flying saucer swooped from the clouds and landed on the dirt runway, raising dust and debris from the force of its engines.

A jumble of thoughts ran through Piper Sands' mind, none of which made sense.

"Our ride," The Caretaker said sardonically.

After the ship touched down, the stairwell descended.

The Caretaker produced a pistol and pointed it at Piper Sands.

"Get aboard."

The two Soviet agents grabbed the young woman and dragged her up the stairs, locking her into one of the honeycombed rooms. After disembarking, the two agents waited at the bottom of the stairs as The Caretaker climbed aboard.

The Caretaker turned to the two agents standing below. "This is where we part ways, gentlemen."

The Caretaker fired two shots from the pistol, killing both agents instantly. He activated the control button to retract the stairwell and joined the pilot on the bridge, taking the empty seat usually occupied by the copilot.

"Welcome aboard, General Lukin," Wes Reed said. He detached the alien looking helmet from his flight suit.

"Will I need a headpiece?" Lukin asked.

"Headpiece? Is that what you Russians call these things?" Reed chuckled. "No, we won't be reaching the kinds of altitudes that require flight suits."

***

"Headpiece?" I said.

Holmes and I had managed to hear all that had transpired between Lukin and the creature piloting.

"As I suspected. Our pilot is no alien. He is wearing a special flight suit designed for high altitude missions. At night those suits can easily be mistaken for something otherworldly."

"You suspected that, did you?"

"At first glance, the sight of those two individuals is arresting. Recall the eyewitness report of the old miner. This picture is becoming much clearer, Watson."

"You still haven't answered my question. Why did you suspect the pilot and copilot were humans?"

"Recall the smoke break and the discarded cigarette you failed to observe by the stairwell. The discarded butt was a Camel, a distinctly American brand. Wouldn't one assume an alien intelligence would have its own brand of cigarettes?"

"You are having a go with me, Holmes. Now that the girl is on board, where is this ship headed?"

"I assume we are headed for the Soviet Union. We are aboard a stolen American experimental craft. No doubt it is a successor to the crashed ship we saw that night in Roswell."

"Holmes, we will be lucky if we are not shot down."

"Yes, we must find a way to force a landing. But first, we must make our presence known to Miss Sands."

Quietly Holmes and I slipped from our hiding place and made our way to the cubicle where Piper Sands was being kept. The lock was a simple slide mechanism. When Holmes and I slipped inside, Miss Sands was seated with a safety harness locked across her chest.

"I do not believe this," Piper Sands said.

"You are welcome," I replied.

"Have you a plan, or will this be another of your improvisations?"

"The numbers are on our side," I said. "There are three of us and two of them."

"Not quite," Holmes replied. "Who among the three of us can fly this craft?"

"Count me out," Agent Sands said.

My flying experience was limited to small planes. This flying behemoth was far beyond my capabilities.

"Then we must overpower The Caretaker and force the pilot to land," said Holmes.

"That means separating the two of them from each other," Agent Sands said.

"Cry out," I said. "Get him back here."

"No, I am not going to do that!"

"We certainly can't scream. As far as they know, you are the only passenger aboard."

"I hate this!"

Piper Sands began crying out at the top of her lungs.

A few moments later, General Lukin slid open the door. Agent Sands was seated, free of her harness. Before Lukin had time to react, Holmes and I leapt upon the General and held him securely. Agent Sands quickly removed Lukin's pistol from the holster inside his coat.

"To the bridge, General. Very carefully," Holmes said.

Piper Sands pressed the pistol against Lukin's back and pushed him forward.

"I take it you are not Jenny Winston," Lukin said.

"My name is Piper Sands. I am a trained agent. Don't think for one moment I will hesitate to pull the trigger."

"I don't doubt that whatsoever. I must congratulate you on the deception."

"Hey, put a sock in it," Agent Sands said.

The four of us moved slowly up the passageway to the bridge.

"What's going on back there?" Lt. Reed called out.

181

Holmes put his hand on Reed's shoulder. "Land the saucer."

Reed turned in his seat.

"They have the gun," Lukin said.

Reed made no attempt to comply. "There is nowhere to put down."

"Land this ship," Holmes repeated.

Lt. Reed chuckled. "What will you do if I don't put down? Will you shoot the General? Be my guest. I don't particularly like him anyway. Or will you shoot me? If you do that, you will be forced to land this ship on your own. It appears you are between a saucer and a hard place."

Lukin dropped his hands. "Hand me the gun, Miss Sands."

Piper Sands turned over the pistol to Lukin.

Lukin and Reed were in control. There was nothing to be done.

"Now, let's see what this baby can really do." Reed said. "Everyone better hold tight."

Reed pulled back on the controls. The ship accelerated rapidly and then went into a steep, dizzying climb.

Reed laughed triumphantly. "I knew it! I knew it could do more!"

The ship's engines whined, as if under an unaccustomed strain.

Holmes, Agent Sands, and I looked at each other anxiously.

"That doesn't sound good," I said.

"Lieutenant, are you sure about this?" Lukin asked.

The engine whine increased to a deafening shrill.

"What is going on?" Agent Sands yelled.

The ship began to vibrate wildly.

Reed fought the controls, attempting to steady the ship.

"Bring it down!" Holmes commanded.

"I am trying!" Reed said, his voice suddenly panicked.

Something deep inside the ship exploded.

"Hang on, we're going down!"

Lukin buckled into the copilot's seat, as Holmes, Agent Sands, and I strapped into the three seats behind the pilot and copilot. We braced ourselves for impact.

The ship descended rapidly through the clouds. Stall alarms sounded, and red lights lit up all over the control panel. Our descent was so dizzying it was impossible to determine where we were. Lt. Reed punched a button to deploy the landing struts. The altimeter indicated we were only a few hundred feet above ground. Suddenly four giant white illuminated faces appeared before us. "Good God," I screamed. We were flying straight toward the great stone faces carved into the side of Mt. Rushmore. The ship made an impossibly sharp turn, flying so close to the monument I was sure the landing struts must have scraped across Washington's forehead. The ship flew up and over the top of the monument, quickly losing altitude. Seconds later it plowed into the earth, skimmed across the ground as a pebble hopping across the surface of a pond, and finally came to a brutally hard stop. Had we not been strapped in, we would most certainly have perished.

For a moment, no one moved. Lt. Reed was the first one to unbuckle. Quickly he pulled a lever, resulting in a blast of compressed air followed by a brief explosion. Lt. Reed had blown open an emergency escape hatch. Grabbing the headpiece with the built-in night vision goggles, he hurled himself through the opening in the side of the saucer and disappeared into the night.

Before the three of us had time to unbuckle our restraints, General Lukin rose from the copilot's seat and turned toward us. He aimed the pistol at Holmes.

"Do not worry, Mr. Holmes. As much as I would like to, I am afraid I do not have the luxury of wasting a single bullet. Once I exit this ship, I may well encounter creatures far more lethal than you."

Lukin disappeared through the escape hatch.

Holmes immediately unbuckled his harness and leapt through the escape hatch to the ground.

"Not without me, you don't," Agent Sands said, flying out of the escape hatch right behind Holmes.

With clouds covering the moon, it was all but impossible to get one's bearings. The intermittent blinking of the ship's emergency lights provided some light. We had crashed in rough terrain.

Peering through the escape hatch, I saw that the ship had crashed on top of a rocky outcropping that couldn't have been more than a mile from the Mt. Rushmore Monument. The lights illuminating the monument glowed in the distance.

"You will never be able to track Lukin in this dark," Agent Sands said. "I am much better suited for this task."

As Holmes peered into the darkness, the blinking landing lights revealed an image. Lukin was only a few yards away, pointing the pistol toward them.

"Watch out!" Agent Sands screamed. She threw herself into Holmes, knocking him to the ground at precisely the same instant a shot rang out, followed by a flash of blue flame. Agent Sands cried out in pain. She collapsed onto the ground next to Holmes. Before Holmes could get to his feet, General Lukin had disappeared into the rocky crags surrounding the crash site.

"Holmes, are you alright?" I called out, exiting through the escape hatch.

"Quick, Watson, Agent Sands has been hit."

Breathlessly I reached Holmes and Agent Sands. The blinking lights revealed a nasty wound to Agent Sands' left shoulder. Thankfully the injury was not life-threatening.

"Steady. It's all right, you'll live."

"Easy for you to say." Agent Sands grimaced in pain with every word she spoke. "Have you ever been shot?"

A painful memory presented itself with such visceral clarity, I felt as if I had been transported to another time. I rose to my feet and walked away.

"Hey! Hey!" Agent Sands called out, "I'm dying here."

I needed air and to clear the flood of memories that had washed over me.

Holmes knelt beside the fallen agent. "He knows," he said gently. "He has seen it; he has experienced it."

A few minutes later, I returned to offer the care I had been trained to provide.

"I am sorry, Dr. Watson. That was thoughtless of me. I didn't know."

"It is already forgotten," I said reassuringly. "We must move you inside. We need protection from the cold and whatever else might be out here at night."

"I assume this craft is equipped with a locator beacon," Holmes said. "I daresay we will be located within a matter of hours."

"What about Lukin and the pilot?" Agent Sands asked. "We can't just let them get away."

"Without the proper equipment and protection, a pursuit in this terrain would be perilous. There is nothing to be done until morning. You need to rest until you can be evacuated."

***

Shortly before daylight, three helicopters landed forming a triangle with the crashed saucer in the middle. A bullhorn demanded the occupants exit with hands in the air. Holmes and I exited the craft. Agent Sands remained inside until a medical team could extract her.

As ordered, Holmes and I held our hands above our heads. Several serious looking soldiers pointed rifles at us.

"Stand down," a familiar voice said.

Colonel Patterson stepped to the fore.

"Nice to see you again, Mr. Holmes," the Colonel said with guarded enthusiasm.

I couldn't help but wonder if Colonel Patterson had turned himself in. If he had, he did not allow. Most likely he had chosen to play the odds.

Holmes filled Patterson in on the details of the crash and the escapes of both Lt. Reed and General Lukin.

"It is doubtful either will get far," Patterson offered. "The terrain here is difficult to navigate on foot."

"Could our escapees have made their way to the monument?" I asked

"Unlikely, Doctor. Were they to reach the monument, there would be nowhere to go. Most likely they both made their way to the highway. I have no doubts we will find them." Colonel Patterson lowered his voice and pulled Holmes aside. "Mr. Holmes, that business about the beauty salon—"

Holmes raised his hand to forestall Colonel Patterson from speaking. "I have one interest and one interest only: that is to ensure the safety of Agent Sands."

"Then I would like to say—"

"Thank you? Colonel, do not misunderstand me. I am most appalled by your conduct. It is impossible to calculate the damage you may have done or the number of lives you have put at risk. The path you choose going forward is your business. Only you can make that choice."

The rebuffed Colonel ordered a pair of soldiers to escort Holmes, Agent Sands, and me to a waiting helicopter. Within minutes we were airborne and headed to Roswell, where the three of us overnighted. The following morning Holmes and I said our goodbyes to Agent Sands, as we were being returned to Washington, and she to a destination undisclosed to us.

Given our brief and turbulent acquaintance with Agent Sands, neither Holmes nor I expected a tearful farewell. We were not disappointed.

"I would like to say it's been fun, but of course we know that's not true. Anyway, thanks for the memories. See you around."

With that less than sincere attempt at sarcasm, Agent Piper Sands exited our lives.

Later that morning Holmes and I returned to Washington, D.C.

CHAPTER 27
Debriefing

Washington D.C.

After arriving in Washington, Holmes and I were joined by Mycroft. We were escorted to the senate office where we had previously met Colonel Hawker. He greeted us warmly, offered coffee, and invited us to sit.

"I am glad to see the senator from Wisconsin will not be joining us," Holmes remarked.

"You rather put him off," the Colonel said. "McCarthy isn't used to being spoken to in such a direct manner."

"Perhaps therein lies the fault. That may be exactly what he needs."

"Regardless, I am glad to see none of you are any worse for wear."

"Certainly not my brother," Holmes quipped. "Ensconced in his office in London, I don't believe Mycroft was ever in danger, were you, brother?"

Mycroft smiled politely, allowing Sherlock's remark to pass without response.

"Now that this business is concluded, no doubt you have many questions."

"I wouldn't go so far as to say concluded. Aren't General Lukin and Lt. Reed still at large?"

"It will only be a matter of time before they are apprehended."

The expression on Holmes's face suggested he had little faith in the Colonel's pronouncement.

"As you may have guessed, Mr. Holmes, what you and Dr. Watson saw that night in Roswell was not a weather balloon."

"Dr. Watson and I have known that fact from the start."

"Well, Holmes knew," I interjected. "I was somewhat slower to arrive at that conclusion."

"What you saw burning to the ground was a prototype of the saucer you prevented the Soviets from stealing. It was an experimental craft under development by a highly classified branch of the Air Force known as Chimera. It began life as a program called Project 1794. Currently three similar projects are underway here in the U.S. and at least one we know of in The Soviet Union. I believe the British also have such a program, is that right, Mycroft?"

Mycroft smiled. "I really couldn't say."

"The craft you saw at Roswell was known as the FD2. It was powered by a since discarded propulsion system. An earlier model, the FD1, was never operational. As I noted during our previous visit, since the end of the war relations with the Soviets have become frosty. Once the Soviets witnessed the power America unleashed on Japan, they committed to a full-scale effort in the development of atomic weaponry and advanced aviation. We are in a virtual race. The FD program is our attempt to advance U.S. technology far beyond anything the Soviets are capable of. Thus far the effort has proven abysmal."

"What about the Soviets?"

"In many respects, the Soviets are Neanderthals; they lack imagination. Originality is not their strong suit. As I noted previously, they are masters of reverse engineering. They are most adept at copying captured technologies, thus the need for self-destruct mechanisms in our aircraft in the event of capture. And they are unmatched when it comes to infiltration and stealing classified documents. Hence our mole problem."

189

"Forgive me, Colonel, but none of this information is new to us. Dr. Watson and I are most anxious to return to London."

"Very well. To make a long story short, their saucer was never going to get off the ground, at least not with the blueprints their mole was passing along. Once we became aware of our leak, we carefully made sure our mole was sending out plans that were useless. The technology they have been receiving is for a propulsion system that will never work. They have wasted years developing a worthless technology."

"Which explains why the Soviets attempted to steal the ship."

"Precisely, Doctor."

Mycroft sighed. "Are we to get the real Roswell story, Colonel? Or will we be sent away once again without knowing the truth?"

"Colonel, if the Soviets' primary goal were the saucer, there would have been no need to apprehend the girl, certainly not after all these years. They, as we, believe there is still something else."

"Quite right, Mr. Holmes. The night of July 7, 1947, the FD2 had taken off from a site near the Dugway Proving Ground in Utah. It flew in a southerly direction that would take it over Roswell, New Mexico. Approximately two hours into the flight, the saucer experienced a catastrophic systems failure. A reserve oxygen tank on board exploded, resulting in a crippling fire. The ship lost altitude and crashed seventy-miles west of Roswell. Both pilots barely escaped with their lives. As thousands had witnessed the fireball falling from the sky, we could hardly deny something had happened.

"Typically, we can dismiss such an occurrence as a meteorite crashing to earth. In this instance there were witnesses. The boy and girl were easy to deal with. They were provided with new identities and relocated. Mr. Carl, on the other hand, proved to be more than a handful. He had gotten on the phone right away with the press, so by the next day the headline read: *RAAF Captures Flying Saucer on Ranch in Roswell Region.* Baring nothing short of a public panic, we needed to come up with a plausible story."

"You believed a flaming weather balloon story would do the job?"

"This is where things get tricky, Doctor. We had known for some time the Soviets were developing their own saucer program. Beyond that, we knew nothing. Perception is important. It was in our best interests to convince the Soviets we were far ahead of them in development. In truth, we had no idea how far along they were. And then Roswell happened. We sure as hell didn't want the Soviets believing we had suffered a major setback, so the boys in propaganda got right to work and cooked up the weather balloon story. The Soviets would expect a cover. The weather balloon story was flimsy enough to satisfy their expectations and plausible enough to convince the public. From the Soviet point of view, the more we denied, the more we had to hide."

"Workers on the inside didn't know the truth?" I asked.

"That was the beauty. We managed to keep a lid on it. It wasn't until some months later we discovered we had one or more moles in our operation. Once we caught on, that is when we began feeding them worthless documents. From a tactical advantage, you always want the enemy to believe they are a step behind."

"Hovering above everything was the old miner and his claims of seeing space aliens," Holmes said.

"Correct. From the moment Abraham Carl made his outrageous claim of seeing two aliens at the crash site, his story took on a bizarre life of its own. Conspiracy stories started popping up everywhere."

"To complicate matters, the boy and girl corroborated Mr. Carl's version of events," Mycroft said.

"That is partly true. What they saw out there that night was a pilot and copilot who had barely escaped with their lives."

"Those were the reptilian creatures," I said.

"Those bizarre flight suits both men were wearing are experimental. They are a full body rubberized material, green in appearance. The helmets have built in flight goggles designed for night vision. In the glow of the fire, they no doubt appeared unearthly."

"We are quite familiar with them," I said.

"Of course. Those details are highly classified."

"Your weather balloon story becomes a ruse to cover an even more outrageous subterfuge," Holmes said.

The Colonel smiled. "Outrageous indeed."

"Your own program which has become an abysmal failure suddenly has new life because the Soviets are convinced the U.S. is in possession of an alien spacecraft and its two occupants."

"The coupe' de grace, Mr. Holmes."

Mycroft nodded approvingly. "Brilliant. Once the story had reached the level of conspiracy, it has been kept alive through continued denials and secrecy."

"The confusion and secrecy the night of the crash, the denials and revised stories, in addition to protecting Jenny Winston have played to our advantage. Clearly Miss Winston had seen something we wished to keep secret. That fueled growing speculation that what had really happened was an alien spacecraft had crashed to earth. And now we are in possession of a technology that reaches beyond our planet."

"Are you not worried word of this deception will get out?" I asked.

"Once a lie takes on a life of its own, it no longer matters."

"Never attempt to win by force what may be won by deception."

"You know your Machiavelli, Doctor. You see, it's all perception. We know their saucer will never fly, and they are convinced we have saucer technology that will. No matter that we both have worthless programs. We win as long as they believe we have something they don't."

"Do you have a position on alien spacecraft, Colonel?" I asked.

"None. As to the sightings that defy explanation, I have no position. Why waste time speculating about things that cannot be proved?"

Colonel Hawker rose and offered his hand to each of us. "On behalf of the President of the United States, our official thanks, gentlemen."

As the three of us prepared to leave, Colonel Hawker reminded us of the confidentiality of the information he had shared with us.

"One last thing, Colonel. What will be the official version of what happened that night near Rapid City?"

"We will let that percolate for a bit, Doctor. I am sure we will come up with something that will keep the Soviets guessing for years."

CHAPTER 28
Loose ends

Nome, Alaska

Saturday nights in Nome during winters were raucous occasions. Locals and visitors crowded into two saloons: The Dexter, built in 1889 by Wyatt Earp, and The Board of Trade, a holdover from the gold rush days. Both saloons were noisy, bawdy, and filled with revelers. Occasionally a fight might break out, but they were quickly settled. Nome more than lived up to its wild and woolly reputation as a final outpost of The Last Frontier.

A lesser known saloon a couple of streets over from Front Street was a broken down old place called The Blowhole. Few tourists found their way to The Blowhole. Mostly it was locals, most of whom preferred to drink alone in a quieter environment.

Over the past few months, Tom Westin had become a regular. Bessie Sampson, owner of the saloon and fulltime bar tender, had come to like Tom.

He was affable enough. Bessie figured he was like many newcomers to Nome; he was seeking a last refuge, a place about as far West as you could go, a place where one could disappear.

Bessie asked few questions, and Tom didn't volunteer much. Over the years dozens of guys like Tom had appeared in Nome. One or two remained. Others eventually disappeared. Tom had once been a professional man. Bessie could tell that. He carried himself well and spoke with an authority that eluded most drifters. Tom had a story worth hearing, but she knew not to ask. Guys such as Tom didn't like questions.

Tom's story began with his name. His name wasn't Thomas Westin, it was Wes Reed. Since ditching the FD3 in the mountains of South Dakota, Reed had been on the run, finally ending up on the western coast of Alaska. He had eluded Sherlock Holmes, the Air Force, and the CIA. Wes Reed was a man without a home or a country.

This was not the way things were supposed to turn out. Reed was supposed to deliver the FD3 to the Soviets, earn the highest of commendations, and then live a life of luxury. Those plans came to a crashing halt. It was easy to blame Sherlock Holmes for the crash, but the truth was he had pushed the FD3 beyond its limits. As far as the Soviets were concerned, Lt. Wes Reed was no longer of use to them. His attempt to defect to seek asylum was rejected. He hadn't delivered as promised. There was nothing else they wanted from him. At home, he was considered a traitor. His trek to Alaska was an attempt to lose himself. He had grown a full beard and let his hair grow long until he no longer bore any resemblance to the clean shaven, crew cut all-American pilot he had once been.

Reed took a stool and tapped on the bar. Instead of his normal glass on tap, Bessie poured a pitcher and walked it along the bar to the man she knew as Tom.

"I didn't order a pitcher," Reed said.

Bessie nodded toward a man seated by himself at one of the tables in the back. "He's buying," she said. She reached under the bar and set down two empty glasses.

Reed turned to the man behind him. His first instinct was to bolt. Then practicality got the better of him. Why bother? There was nowhere to run to in Nome. Your choice was frozen tundra or frozen sea.

Reed carried the two glasses and pitcher to the table.

"Small world," he said, pouring two glasses of beer.

"The beard suits you," Mark Daniels said.

That night at Buffalo Gap, South Dakota, Reed's orders had been to walk Daniels into the woods and kill him. The fewer witnesses, the better. Reed couldn't bring himself to do that. He and Daniels had been partners too long. Instead, he had knocked his partner unconscious. Once the Soviets were in possession of the ship, why would they care what had happened to Mark Daniels?

"How did you find me?"

"You talked about seeing Nome once. You don't fly with a guy for four years without learning something about him. It was worth a shot."

"Yeah, I suppose." Reed stared into his beer. He was at the end of the line and he was tired. "Are you here to arrest me?"

"If that's what it takes."

"Does that mean I have a choice?"

"We all have choices. Sometimes you make good choices, sometimes you don't."

"What is mine?"

"You finish your beer, and then you walk out on the ice headed west."

The night was clear and cold, the temperature well below zero. A belly full of beer would make things easier.

The two men finished the pitcher. Daniels did not ask Reed why he had done it, and Reed didn't volunteer his reason.

Before leaving, Reed tipped Bessie with all the money he had on him.

He and Daniel's exchanged a farewell nod.

The Northern Lights were out and dancing, illuminating the ice pack covering the Bering Sea. Wes Reed pulled his parka tight and began his walk west.

***

Kasputin Yar

The decorators finished ahead of schedule. Yuri Olenev could not have been more pleased. He was anxious to move into Sokolov's old office and to begin work as the new head of Kasputin Yar. Promoted to the rank of major, Olenev had been amply rewarded for his testimony against Major Dmitri Sokolov. Kremlin officials had been sympathetic to Olenev's story that he had been a helpless underling doing the bidding of his treacherous superior. Threats of demotion and possibly even death had prohibited the young lieutenant from speaking up earlier.

Olenev's first order of business was to kill The Olympus Project. Too much time and too much money had already been wasted on that white elephant. Time to look ahead. There had been talk of launching an orbiting satellite. Major Yuri Olenev was ready to assert Soviet dominance in the race to space.

***

Moscow

Four Soviet agents broke down the door of the tiny apartment and immediately set about destroying the place. A short time later Arkady Shubin arrived. Although Shubin no longer had direct authority over them, the agents tossed the apartment as a favor to their former boss.

"Well?"

"Nothing," one of the agents said.

"What about the girl?" Shubin demanded.

"By the look of things, she's cleared out. Long gone."

"Can you find her?" Shubin asked.

"No, we have done all we can. It is up to the new First Chief Directorate."

The four agents left Shubin alone to walk through the shambles of what had once been the home of Tatiana Andreyev. He sat on the small sofa and pushed his hands through his thinning hair. How had this happened? Why had that sniveling wretch been so disloyal? He looked up. On the mantle was a small, framed photograph. Shubin rose and held the photo frame in his hand. It was a photograph of Tatiana Andreyev, smiling. Was it a smile of defiance, ridicule, victory? Written across the photo were the words *To Arkady, With Love.*

***

Yaniv

It wasn't Siberia, but it might as well be. A taxi dumped Dmitri Sokolov and his belongings in front of the ruin that had been his home as a boy. He had been told he should feel lucky he was not being sent to a gulag. What would have been the difference he wondered? What kind of life would he make for himself here? He sat on his suitcase and lit a cigarette. Had he been so stupid, so arrogant to believe he could have been passed top-secret plans for years without the Americans catching on? When had they discovered the truth? The truth. What about the American saucer program? Had it been a failure from the start? And Roswell, damn Roswell! What was the truth? There was plenty of blame to be spread around, but it was the pompous ass Shubin who had created most of his problems. And for what? It was all over that silly English girl he had met in Paris. His harebrained scheme to use Sherlock Holmes as a means of getting even with his brother had led to this. He should have left well enough alone and focused solely on the Winston girl. Yet even that was all bollocks, as the English would say. The Soviets had been played for fools from the start. Operation Dead Loop he chuckled to himself. More like Operation Dead End.

***

Bel Air, Los Angeles

A portly man sat at his writing desk in his home office absorbed with a newspaper article. It was the story of a shooting and a mysterious crash in the mountains near Mt. Rushmore. The man removed a pair of scissors from his desk drawer and carefully cut out the article, which he then placed in a folder stuffed with various newspaper clippings.

A voice called to him from an adjoining room. "Alfred, tea time!"

The man didn't respond. He was lost in thought imagining a scene based upon the story he had just read.

***

London

As Tatiana Andreyev arrived on the platform at Elephant & Castle, she was taken aback. She had been prepared for a crowd of waiting passengers. There were almost no passengers waiting for the next train. Oh well, she said to herself, I will have a train to myself. She was positively giddy over the thought of being in London and seeing the sights. It was so liberating to be free of the cold and gloom of Moscow and the prison basement she had been working in for years. Moscow was home. It was all she had ever known. But now she would never return. She had been given the rare opportunity of a new life and she had every intention of making the best of it. She had gone to the British consulate in Moscow and presented herself as the one who had dropped the unaddressed envelope into the British ambassador's letterbox. The ambassador had been more than willing to help.

A sudden blast of wind pushed through the tunnel, followed by the light of a train entering the station. The steel wheels screeched as the train came to a stop. Tatiana waited for passengers to disembark before entering the carriage. She chose a seat at the end of the carriage. There was only one other passenger, a young woman sitting at the opposite end, reading a London newspaper. Tatiana glanced up at the station map. She would disembark at the next stop. The doors hissed closed, and the train pulled away from the station on its way to the next stop. Tatiana couldn't help but smile. She was scared for herself, but it was a good kind of scared. She had no idea what the future had in store. Her life was now in the hands of chance. As the tube train slowed on its approach to the next station, Tatiana rose and held onto the support rail by the door. As the doors hissed open, the girl at the opposite end of the carriage, put down her paper. She smiled at Tatiana, as if to say hello. Tatiana returned the young woman's smile and stepped onto the platform. Suddenly she froze. Her mind whirred through its vast photo file. She turned back just as the doors closed. Tatiana hammered on the glass and waved frantically. The tube train began pulling away.

The young woman on the train smiled again, only this time curiously. The girl on the platform seemed to know her. What did it matter if she didn't know the girl on the platform? Ellen Sharpe waved anyway.

New Mexico

BY THE AUTHORITY OF THE HOUSE OF
REPRESENTATIVES OF THE
CONGRESS OF THE UNITED STATES OF AMERICA

To Victor R. Cherepanov:
        You are hereby commanded to appear before a sub-committee of the Un-American Activities Committee of the House of Representatives of the United States.

The agent who went by the name Cherepanov stared at the summons in disbelief. His hand shook so violently he could hardly read what was written. How had this happened? Had his cover been blown? Why hadn't his calls been returned? Wasn't there somebody inside to protect him? Why hadn't the Soviets responded to his calls for help?
        He read the letter again. He had one week. In one week he would have to appear before Joseph McCarthy.

***

Nice, France

Ariel Starling missed her old name. It would take time to get used to her new one. It was part of the job. She had been Jenny Winston, Clare Simmons, and Piper Sands. Lying on a chaise in the lazy afternoon sun on the French Riviera, the job wasn't without certain advantages. How long she would have to remain a part of the identity protection program was anyone's guess. Today was her birthday. She had reached a birthday milestone, not her twenty-fourth birthday as the

Americans believed, but her thirtieth. Ariel was much younger looking than her age allowed. It was precisely because of her youthful appearance and resemblance to Jenny Winston that the Americans had been persuaded that she could pass for Jenny. The Americans had no idea they were training a seasoned British agent. After the mess created by Roswell, the Americans were more than willing to allow the British to handle all matters related to arranging a new identity for Piper Sands. As far as they were concerned, they had one less matter to clean up.

As Ariel had yet to make new friends in Nice, she would be celebrating alone.

Friends would come, but for the time a birthday alone felt bittersweet.

"May I?"

A shadow fell across Ariel. The man in the preposterous hat was holding an ice bucket and a bottle of champagne.

"One really shouldn't celebrate one's birthday alone," he said.

Ariel smiled and gestured for Mycroft Holmes to take the chaise beside her.

"Thank you," she said. "You have made my day."

"The least I can do." Mycroft popped open the champagne and poured two glasses. "Her Majesty sends you birthday greetings."

"*Her* Majesty? That's right, I almost forgot. I wasn't there for the coronation. Does she really send birthday greetings?"

"No, not really. But I believe I may speak on her behalf. Your nation owes you a debt of gratitude."

Ariel rubbed the fresh scar on her right shoulder. "I don't know about that, but your brother does. How is Sherlock?"

"Well."

"Of course, I owe him for saving my life, so I suppose we are even. I should like to thank him. I never did that properly."

"I am sure he knows."

"Will you ever tell the Americans?"

"About?"

"Me."

"Oh, you mean how you were one of the moles they could never find?"

"Not that, silly goose. I am speaking of my birthday. You won't tell them how old I really am, will you? I rather enjoyed reliving my twenties."

"Your secret is safe with me." Mycroft tapped his glass against Ariel's. "Cheers!"

CHAPTER 29
Thereby hangs a tale

London

Following our return to London, life returned to normal. Holmes and I settled into our familiar routines. I scaled back my medical practice to devote additional time to my writing.

Holmes would have none of it.

"We both know very well why you have reduced your workload."

"I believe I have been entirely clear."

"Not at all, Watson. Miss Terry is a charming companion. You do her a disservice by pretending she is not the reason for your change in schedule. I am least qualified to give advice regarding the fairer sex, but you really must come to terms with your feelings and hers."

Holmes knew me well. It was true. I was quite taken with Miss Terry and she with me. Our experience in New York had created an emotional intimacy between us we may not have otherwise achieved. She had a recollection of the telephone call she had been forced to make and the humiliation that followed; she did not know the rest. I did not tell her I had seen her in the hotel room that night. I allowed I had been snatched before entering the hotel.

As I found more reasons to enjoy the company of Eden Terry, I communicated less frequently with Holmes. On my last visit to 221B, Holmes allowed he was restless and had decided to go on holiday. It was a spur of the moment decision.

"Most unlike you, Holmes," I observed.

"Agreed, but I believe I have reached a point in my life where I may be unpredictable, n'est-ce pas?"

"Of course, but where will you go?" I asked, hardly convinced Holmes was being entirely open with me.

"Go?" Holmes asked. "I have yet to decide."

"It bears repeating: most unlike you, Holmes."

Holmes remained vague, assuring me postcards would follow.

***

Paris

I was to learn Holmes had made for Paris. He established a temporary residence at the Caron de Beaumarchais. How long he would stay, he could not say. The hotel management was delighted to have a guest of such celebrity. Mr. Holmes could stay whatever length of time he wished.

Holmes embraced the role of tourist, visiting galleries and sights throughout Paris. His visits were always to different locations bustling with visitors. His only routine was to take coffee every day at The Esplanade, a quaint outdoor café below The Eiffel Tower.

On Holmes's eighth day in Paris, a visitor joined him for coffee. The visitor did not ask to join Holmes. He sat, uninvited.

Having immersed himself in a copy of Le Figaro, Holmes folded the newspaper and placed it on the table.

"General Lukin."

"You are not surprised to see me, Mr. Holmes."

"I thought you would never make contact. I have positively run out of sights to see in this glorious city."

"How long have you known?"

"Since the day I returned to London."

"Ah yes, your Baker Street misfits."

"As a consulting detective, one is used to being followed. A competent tail is often difficult to spot. They are subtle in ways the thugs you surround yourself with are not. It has been my experience that Soviet goons are clumsy, stupid, and lazy." Holmes took note of his surroundings. "Unless I am mistaken, you are in the company of four of those thugs now."

"Most observant. I gather your routine has been designed to lure me to this very open and public setting."

"I much prefer a bright and sunny location to a dark alley."

"Where one would normally expect to find Sherlock Holmes lurking in the shadows."

Holmes snapped his fingers for a waiter.

"Another espresso, steaming this time. Anything for you, General?"

"No!"

The waiter nodded and hurried away.

"Are you always so cavalier? You do not fear for your life, Mr. Holmes?"

"Should I? You had your opportunity to kill me at the crash site and you chose not to. From the beginning of your operation I have been a target. I presume I still am. Or is your interest in me now personal?"

"You have a well-deserved reputation for arrogance, Mr. Holmes."

"General, you surely have not come to Paris to insult me."

"I take it the young lady survived."

"Recovered nicely."

"She mistakenly assumed I was aiming for you, when in fact she was my target. Had she not lunged toward you the moment I fired, she would have been shot through the heart."

"Agent Sands posed no threat to you."

"Had the two of you remained on the ship, shooting her would not have been necessary. A young woman with her training and stamina could have easily tracked me down. I couldn't take that chance."

"That will no doubt prove a comfort to her. But tell me, General, how do you envision this little scene concluding?"

"I give you something to make you sleep, and then we whisk you away in a wheelchair. It is not uncommon for a tourist to fall ill."

"Now that Arkady Shubin is no longer director of Foreign Intelligence, am I to assume revenge is no longer a consideration?"

Lukin stirred the air with his hand. "A little perhaps. We would like to embarrass the British government. What better way than by apprehending The Great Detective? That is what they call you, do they not?"

"You embarrass me. You must be a fan."

"I see your intent is to get under my skin. You have succeeded. Our tête-à-tête has come to an end."

The waiter from whom Holmes ordered the espresso approached the table. Holmes took note of the positions of Lukin's men and the timing of the lifts that ferried visitors to the top of The Eiffel Tower. His means of escape would be limited to a single well-timed choice.

Lukin slipped his hand into his pocket.

As the waiter leaned forward to place the tray, Holmes slapped the tray with his hand. The tray and the scalding coffee hit General Lukin in the face. Lukin howled in pain.

Holmes bolted from the table and dashed toward the tower lifts. Lukin and his henchmen gave chase. The gate of the awaiting lift closed before his pursuers were close enough to grab Holmes.

Lukin watched the lift ascend, his face blistering from the hot coffee.

"One of you come with me. The rest of you cover the lifts," Lukin ordered. "Holmes has no other way down. Make sure no one gets on. Tell them a deranged man poses a threat."

Lukin and one of his thugs boarded the next lift for the second level of the tower. There he ordered all occupants out. "Police business," he said.

Of the two lifts that accessed the top of the tower, one was closed for maintenance.

"Guard the stairs," Lukin commanded. Once the operative lift returned to the second level, he entered the lift that would take him to the top of the tower and Sherlock Holmes.

After Holmes arrived at the top level, he noted visitor traffic was unusually light. A pair of lovers and a husband and wife with two children were the only ones present.

At best Holmes had less than two minutes to formulate a plan. The gate to the closed lift was padlocked. A warning sign was strung across the lift gate. The out of order lift sat immobile hundreds of feet below on the second level of the tower.

"Quickly, you must leave now!" Holmes ordered. "It is an emergency."

"Should we wait for the lift?" The husband asked.

"No time. This is a very serious situation. Take the stairs down to the next level."

Immediately the young couple and the family hurried to the stair entrance.

Holmes's mind raced. "Wait!" He commanded. "Hairpins, I need hairpins. Two."

The young woman shrugged. She didn't use hairpins. She and her boyfriend hurried down the stairs.

The mother pushed her two children and husband into the stairwell. "Here!" She cried. She pulled two hairpins from her hair.

"Go. Hurry!" Holmes ordered.

Satisfied the young family was out of danger, Holmes ripped the warning sign from the gate. Then he went to work on the lock. He expertly manipulated the hairpins until the lock clicked open. He slid open the gate and threw the notice and lock into the maw of the shaft. He closed the gate as the lift bearing General Lukin arrived.

The general stepped out, pleased to see he and Holmes were the only two occupants of the upper most level.

Holmes stood with his back to the out of order lift. He had already determined Lukin would not use a gun. His specialty was syringes.

Lukin reached for his inside pocket and removed the syringe he had been reaching for when Holmes doused him with scalding hot coffee.

"That burn looks painful. You really should put something on it."

"Is this what you had in mind, Mr. Holmes? Have I fallen into your trap? Do you think a scalding hot cup of coffee will dissuade me from my purpose?"

Lukin pulled the protective shield from the syringe.

"As an Englishman, it is in my nature to maintain an appropriate social distance. Your plan to inject me with that syringe will necessitate that we stand uncomfortably close."

"Be assured, Mr. Holmes, I have plenty of experience dealing with reluctant patients. Are we finished now? I have had enough of your foolish babble intended to distract me. If you imagine reinforcements are on their way to save you, you are mistaken."

Lukin moved toward Holmes.

"I must commend you, General, you are a worthy—" Holmes abruptly stopped speaking and averted his eyes from Lukin's with a slight nod of the head at something over the General's shoulder.

In that time-tested and obvious ploy to distract, Lukin fell for the gambit. The instant Lukin glanced over his shoulder, Holmes grabbed the forearm of the hand holding the syringe and violently pulled Lukin toward him as his other hand yanked open the gate. Unable to stop his forward motion, Lukin teetered precariously on the edge of the elevator shaft. His arms flailed wildly in a useless attempt to maintain his balance. In the final moment of his life, Lukin glanced at Holmes with utter incomprehension.

"Perhaps, this is the reason I am known as The Great Detective," Holmes said coldly.

Lukin's scream lasted but a few seconds.

A flock of pigeons alit from The Eiffel Tower.

Holmes knew the henchmen would be long gone by the time he reached ground level. They would be fearing for their lives, not from Holmes or the French police, but from the Soviets.

In the days to follow, all manner of accusations would be exchanged regarding the death of the Soviet operative known as The Caretaker. The British would be blamed, and then the French. The Soviets would promise a thorough and transparent investigation. After several months, the Soviets would conclude their investigation claiming to know nothing of this man known as The Caretaker. He was an independent actor.

Eventually, another sociopath would take Lukin's place.

British and French authorities wrapped up their investigations of Holmes in short order. Mycroft had seen to it that his brother would face no further scrutiny. Sherlock Holmes was free to resume his holiday.

Some weeks later I received a postcard posted from Italy. It was from Holmes, assuring me of his good spirits and good health. His return to London was imminent. But first he had a piece of business to take care of. He was pursuing a lead regarding an old flame.

"I'll be damned," I said.

John H. Watson, London, 1955

Also by Michael Druce

Sherlock Holmes and The Portal of Time

Only one man can change the outcome of World War II—Professor Moriarty. And only one man can stop him—Sherlock Holmes. In a breakneck race through time, Holmes and Watson must follow Moriarty eighteen years into the future to prevent him from helping the Germans develop the atomic bomb. With the fate of the world hanging in the balance, Holmes and Watson join forces with H.G. Wells, his wife Jane, and Albert Einstein in a life and death struggle on the eve of World War II.

www.mxpublishing.com

Also from MX Publishing

MX Publishing is the world's largest specialist Sherlock Holmes publisher, with over a hundred titles and fifty authors creating the latest in Sherlock Holmes fiction and non-fiction.

From traditional short stories and novels to travel guides and quiz books, MX Publishing cater for all Holmes fans.

The collection includes leading titles such as *Benedict Cumberbatch In Transition* and *The Norwood Author* which won the 2011 Howlett Award (Sherlock Holmes Book of the Year).

MX Publishing also has one of the largest communities of Holmes fans on Facebook with regular contributions from dozens of authors.

www.mxpublishing.com

Also from MX Publishing

The Detective and The Woman Series

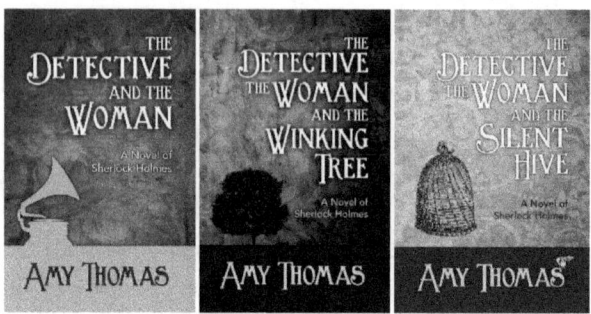

The Detective and The Woman
The Detective, The Woman and The Winking Tree
The Detective, The Woman and The Silent Hive

"The book is entertaining, puzzling and a lot of fun. I believe the author has hit on the only type of long-term relationship possible for Sherlock Holmes and Irene Adler. The details of the narrative only add force to the romantic defects we expect in both of them and their growth and development are truly marvelous to watch. This is not a love story. Instead, it is a coming-of-age tale starring two of our favorite characters."
Philip K Jones

www.mxpublishing.com

Also from MX Publishing

When the papal apartments are burgled in 1901, Sherlock Holmes is summoned to Rome by Pope Leo XII. After learning from the pontiff that several priceless cameos that could prove compromising to the church, and perhaps determine the future of the newly unified Italy, have been stolen, Holmes is asked to recover them. In a parallel story, Michelangelo, the toast of Rome in 1501 after the unveiling of his Pieta, is commissioned by Pope Alexander VI, the last of the Borgia pontiffs, with creating the cameos that will bedevil Holmes and the papacy four centuries later. For fans of Conan Doyle's immortal detective, the game is always afoot. However, the great detective has never encountered an adversary quite like the one with whom he crosses swords in "The Vatican Cameos."

"An extravagantly imagined and beautifully written Holmes story"
(Lee Child, NY Times Bestselling author, Jack Reacher series)

Also from MX Publishing

Sherlock Holmes novellas in verse

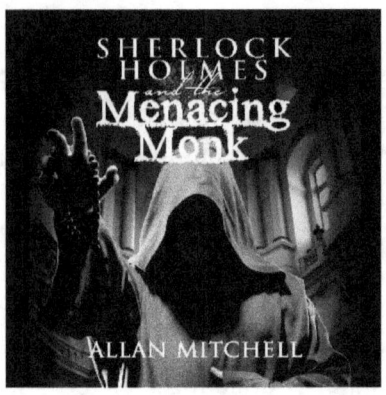

All four
novellas have
been released
also in audio
format with
narration by
Steve White

Sherlock Holmes and The Menacing Moors
Sherlock Holmes and The Menacing Metropolis
Sherlock Holmes and The Menacing Melbournian
Sherlock Holmes and The Menacing Monk

*"The story is really good and the Herculean effort it must
have been to write it all in verse—well, my hat is off to you,
Mr. Allan Mitchell! I wouldn't dream of seeing such work
get less than five plus stars from me…"* **The Raven**

Also from MX Publishing

The Conan Doyle Notes (The Hunt For Jack The Ripper) "Holmesians have long speculated on the fact that the Ripper murders aren't mentioned in the canon, though the obvious reason is undoubtedly the correct one: even if Conan Doyle had suspected the killer's identity he'd never have considered mentioning it in the context of a fictional entertainment. Ms Madsen's novel equates his silence with that of the dog in the night-time, assuming that Conan Doyle did know who the Ripper was but chose not to say – which, of course, implies that good old stand-by, the government cover-up. It seems unlikely to me that the Ripper was anyone famous or distinguished, but fiction is not fact, and "The Conan Doyle Notes" is a gripping tale, with an intelligent, courageous and very likable protagonist in DD McGil."
The Sherlock Holmes Society of London

www.mxpublishing.com